AV
JK ✓

"You're an amazingly selfless and beautiful woman, Molly Murphy."

"I don't think so…"

Without warning, she felt Ryan's mouth drawing closer to hers, cutting short her words as her own lips instinctively reached up to accept his kiss. Then she stopped. She froze and moved away.

"I'm sorry," Ryan said, moving away. "I overstepped the line. Please forgive me, Molly."

Molly couldn't speak for a moment. She wanted to kiss him but she couldn't. Something was holding her back. And that something was her past.

D1018479

Dear Reader,

Have you ever had one of those days when you need everything to go right…and instead everything goes wrong? Horribly wrong. Well, that's just what happens to anesthesia nurse Molly Murphy on the first day of her new job. A job she needs so desperately to ensure that she and her younger brother, Tommy, are not thrown to the curb by her landlord. Or worse, seduced by his lecherous son, who is more than happy if she pays her rent in another way.

Dumped at the altar and left destitute, Molly Murphy has sworn off men. They bring heartache in spades, and she is tired of shoveling her way through life. She knows only too well that Prince Charming doesn't exist.

Dr. Ryan McFetridge is a handsome, single GP who needs an efficient temp office manager. He doesn't need a girlfriend or a wife because he is too busy taking care of his patients and his nineteen-year-old daughter. A relationship is the last thing he needs. Deceived in the past, he wants uncomplicated flings with women who do not have to be home by the stroke of midnight.

There will be challenges, tears and, above all else, honesty needed if this unlikely couple is to open their hearts, let go of the past and find their fairy-tale happily-ever-after.

Susanne

THE DOCTOR'S CINDERELLA

———

SUSANNE HAMPTON

HARLEQUIN® MEDICAL ROMANCE™

If you purchased this book without a cover you should be aware
that this book is stolen property. It was reported as "unsold and
destroyed" to the publisher, and neither the author nor the
publisher has received any payment for this "stripped book."

Recycling programs
for this product may
not exist in your area.

ISBN-13: 978-1-335-66363-4

The Doctor's Cinderella

First North American Publication 2018

Copyright © 2018 by Susanne Panagaris

All rights reserved. Except for use in any review, the reproduction or
utilization of this work in whole or in part in any form by any electronic,
mechanical or other means, now known or hereafter invented, including
xerography, photocopying and recording, or in any information storage
or retrieval system, is forbidden without the written permission of the
publisher, Harlequin Enterprises Limited, 22 Adelaide St. West, 40th Floor,
Toronto, Ontario M5H 4E3, Canada.

This is a work of fiction. Names, characters, places and incidents are
either the product of the author's imagination or are used fictitiously,
and any resemblance to actual persons, living or dead, business
establishments, events or locales is entirely coincidental.

This edition published by arrangement with Harlequin Books S.A.

For questions and comments about the quality of this book,
please contact us at CustomerService@Harlequin.com.

® and TM are trademarks of Harlequin Enterprises Limited or its
corporate affiliates. Trademarks indicated with ® are registered in the
United States Patent and Trademark Office, the Canadian Intellectual
Property Office and in other countries.

Printed in U.S.A.

Books by Susanne Hampton

Harlequin Medical Romance

Christmas Miracles in Maternity

White Christmas for the Single Mom

The Monticello Baby Miracles

Twin Surprise for the Single Doc

Midwives On-Call

Midwife's Baby Bump

Unlocking the Doctor's Heart
Back in Her Husband's Arms
Falling for Dr. December
A Baby to Bind Them
A Mommy to Make Christmas

Visit the Author Profile page
at Harlequin.com.

To my father.
You gave me unconditional love.
You encouraged me to pursue my dreams.
You wanted me to be the best version of myself.
You are my hero looking down from heaven.

And to Helen Mckerral for encouraging me
to write this story and believing that I could
do it justice. Thank you.

Praise for
Susanne Hampton

"*White Christmas for the Single Mom* is wonderful
medical drama with a soul that made my little
reader heart explode with every emotion I
experienced."

—*Goodreads*

CHAPTER ONE

MOLLY MURPHY WAS sad and irritated in equal amounts and she was barely awake. Clanging sounds followed by thuds in the street outside had woken her from a deep and much-needed sleep. Soft frown lines formed on her forehead as she rolled over and pulled the pillow around her ears but the harsh sounds continued. She gave up trying to block them out. The pillow was far too thin and no match for the noise.

It was officially the first day of winter in Australia and unrelenting rain had been teeming down for five days straight. Molly could hear that hadn't abated overnight. The tin roof was still being hammered by the downpour but the other sounds were even louder. She rubbed her eyes, then closed them again as she contemplated whether she should get up. Her alarm hadn't sounded so she decided to stay put.

Pleasant dreams were hard to come by for

Molly and she wasn't happy that one had been cut short as it had been far better than her reality of late. As she lay in the cosiness of her bed, her immediate recollection was a little scattered but it had included a sun-drenched, sandy beach, a cocktail with a tiny paper umbrella…and no overdue bills on the kitchen counter.

Suddenly her musing stopped as she peeked through her heavy eyelids in the direction of the window. Winter sunlight was streaming in through kinks in the ageing venetian blinds. The intensity of the light saw irritation turn to panic. Even half-asleep Molly knew her room should not have been that brightly lit at six-thirty. It was the first of June. It was officially winter and it should have been dark outside. Feeling her heart begin to pick up speed, she anxiously reached over for her mobile phone on the nightstand. The screen was black. The phone was flat. The alarm was never going to sound. She tried to focus on the clock hanging in the hallway opposite her door. It was almost eight o'clock. She had overslept by an hour and a half.

'Oh, God…no, no, no, not today…'

Her reality was now even further from dreams of a cocktail on a beach.

Molly sat bolt upright in her bed. Only to

collapse back down again in pain. Her head had collided with the ridiculously placed wooden bookcase that jutted out from the vinyl-covered bedhead. Hideous decorating from the sixties had sent her crashing back onto her pillow. Her knees instinctively lifted up to her chin and she rocked as her fingers gently rubbed the smarting skin underneath her mop of messy curls. Through tired and now-watering eyes, she looked upwards at the heavy wooden structure inconveniently protruding only twelve inches over the top of her bed.

'Damn you,' she spat as a few tears began spilling from her eyes and trickling down her cheeks. Molly surmised her crying was partly from the shock of hitting something so hard, partly from the pain that followed and maybe more than a little from what had led her to be sleeping in a bed with such a goddamn ugly bedhead.

Love. Naive, stupid love.

Molly had lost almost everything because of it.

And she still blamed herself.

But the new, resilient, heart-of-stone Molly Murphy would never fall in love again. Not ever. It hurt too much.

Taking a deep breath and wiping away the tears with the back of her hand, she attempted to calm herself. She didn't have time for self-pity, not even a few minutes of it. She had to put on her big-girl panties and get going because she was running late. Very late. And since she had been sleeping in the same bed for close to a year with the horrific bookcase bedhead hovering over her, she had no choice but to assume at least part of the responsibility. Each time she had knocked her head on the oak eyesore, and there had been numerous times, she had vowed not to do it again. But then, half-asleep, she would go and *do it again*. If the house were hers, she would have ripped the monstrosity of a bedhead from the wall. But as a tenant she had no choice but to be the victim of it. And that unfortunately happened with annoying and painful regularity.

Insomnia had been her only bedtime companion since her fiancé had disappeared into the night without warning. He had just scribbled a five-line note that, after stripping away the narcissistic wordsmithing, had explained nothing. It had also provided Molly with no inkling of the mess that she would be left to face alone, including the last-minute cancellation of their winter wedding.

Since that dreadful day she had been tossing and turning alone in her bed, so the evening before the anniversary of the day on which she should have been walking down the aisle, she had gone to her room early. Trying desperately not to throw herself a full-blown pity party, she had listened to her female empowerment playlist on her mobile phone. Hours of the edgy, no-holds-barred lyrics had finally allowed her to fall asleep under the security of the heavy woollen blankets. And had also allowed her phone battery to go flat. If it hadn't been for the relentless clanging of each bin being emptied into the truck then dropped back to the kerb in her narrow rain-soaked street, she might well have slept until midday. The sound of the trains shuttling past so close to her tiny home that her windows rattled had become white noise over the months and something she could easily sleep through. And she now knew the rain pelting down had joined the same category.

The sharp pain on the crown of her head quickly replaced the threat of melancholy thoughts as she climbed hurriedly but still a little gun-shy from underneath the weight of her warm covers. Still mumbling to herself, Molly switched to fight-or-flight mode as her feet touched the chilly floorboards of her bedroom. The tiny home was close to ninety years old and there were little gaps between the aged planks that allowed a draft into her room anywhere in the house where there wasn't time-weary linoleum. But that morning Molly barely noticed the icy landing. She was in too much of a rush.

There was no time to wash her hair. In fact, there was barely enough time to run a brush through the short curly brunette bob as she ran into her tiny bathroom, jumped under a two-minute shower and then dressed in the semi-darkness of her room. Molly knew there was a hard rubbish collection as well as the bins so the council workers would be collecting the bins on both sides of the street and she didn't want to be their early morning floor show, so she hurriedly pulled the curtains closed over the broken blinds.

Reaching for the light switch, she found the single light globe hovering over her head had blown. Mentally taking stock of the morning up to that point, she decided it was disastrous and apparently getting worse by the second. The clock was ticking. The next bus would be pulling up at the nearest bus stop in eight minutes and she couldn't even resort to the flashlight on her phone.

She pulled a skirt and shirt from the wardrobe, hoping they matched or at least came close, and her fingers felt around manically under her bed for her shoes. She didn't have time to open the curtains and begin her search. Her heart was beating a little faster than usual as her anxiety levels had peaked. She needed this job as she had few savings left and she had health insurance due the following week, along with the rent and utilities. Molly was well aware that her landlord was not the understanding type. His eldest son and right-hand man, Joel, on the other hand, would offer leniency, accepting part-payment at a price Molly would never pay. He knew she was single, struggling financially and he made his terms very clear. The very thought made her skin crawl and her stomach heave. She would rather live in a tent than give in to him.

Still shuddering with the revolting image of Joel when he delivered his disgusting proposition, Molly raced into the kitchen, on the way calling out to her younger brother, Tommy. Quickly she realised with the lack of a response that he had already left for work. She was grateful that at least one of them had headed off on time. After grabbing a muesli bar from the pantry for breakfast and tossing the phone charger into her bag, Molly threw on her heavy overcoat and hurriedly closed and locked the front door behind her. She navigated puddles down the cracked pathway of her yard, noticing the grass on either side was covered with a layer of overnight frost. Winter was there to stay, she decided as she ran in the rain-dampened cold morning air for the bus stop only two streets from hers. She had forgotten her gloves so she secured her bag on her shoulder and pushed her hands inside the deep pockets of her heavy overcoat. She had, according to her calculations, two minutes to make it to the stop.

Still catching her breath as she rounded the corner, Molly watched in horror as the fully laden bus pulled away from the kerb. The windows were foggy with the warm breath of the early morning passengers all cramped inside and holding on to the ceiling straps so they didn't lose their footing as the bus muscled its way into the fast flow of traffic. She stopped in her tracks, huffing and puffing and staring helplessly as it drove away. Never before had she wished so much to be crammed uncomfortably against strangers as she did at that moment. Never before had she worried that two minutes could potentially change the course of her life and put her on the unemployment line.

A feeling of resignation that she had no power to change her sad state of affairs washed over her as she walked towards the bus stop and waited in line for the next bus. She could make it to her temp assignment if the next one was on time, but if it was late then she too would be late and there was the risk that the practice would call the agency and request another temp and she would be down a month's steady income.

That couldn't happen, she thought as she looked around her at the crowd building in anticipation of the arrival of the next early morning bus. Was she the only one who had slept in and was at risk of eviction if the bus was late? Was she the only person whose life had been tipped upside down and had still not righted itself, despite how hard and how long she tried to get herself back on track? Was she the only one who couldn't afford to hail a cab even if she could get one to stop, which she doubted as they would all be taken on a day like this?

The cold breeze gained intensity, cutting through Molly's coat. She pulled her arms closer to her body and tried to stop the shivers taking over. Chilled to her core, and waiting in line for a bus that she prayed would arrive in time, she looked around at the others also huddled around the bus shelter. There were schoolchildren of various ages and heights in different uniforms but all with raincoats and backpacks; office workers with briefcases; a construction worker in his high-vis vest, carrying his metal lunch box and hard hat; and an elderly couple holding gloved hands, their faces a little contorted by the frosty elements but no doubt, Molly thought, warmed by each other's company. She had no such comfort or company.

Within a few minutes, and with no warning, the ominous grey clouds that were threatening a downpour opened their floodgates. Hurriedly Molly reached back for her hood but there wasn't one. Both of her black winter overcoats were on the hall stand and naturally, in keeping with the tone of the morning, she had chosen the coat without a hood. There was no room as her fellow travellers rushed for the already oversubscribed shelter and moments later it became obvious her umbrella was not in her oversized handbag.

It couldn't get worse, Molly decided. She would arrive resembling a drowned rat and more than likely late for a much-needed new job. She allowed herself a few seconds to once again indulge in the state of her life, which at that moment was quite dreadful. Then she took a deep breath and settled her thoughts. Until she looked down at her rain-splattered feet and almost laughed out loud.

'Really? Who does that?' she mumbled. With the noise of the heavy traffic rushing by on the wet roads no one could have heard her mutterings but Molly no longer cared if they had. It didn't bother her if the world thought she was mad because at that moment she felt awfully close to it anyway. In her fluster and the darkness of her tiny bedroom, she had slipped into odd ballet flats. One navy and the other black. The black one had a small velvet bow and Molly felt quite certain that unless her work colleagues were short-sighted they would notice. It would be an embarrassing beginning. Then something deep inside reminded her that it was the beginning of something new. A new start, she thought. A rebooting of her life, she told herself as the rain trickled down her temples and inside the collar of her coat.

With that thought, her soggy chin raised a little. It was the beginning of Molly Murphy's new life. The old debts were finally paid in full. It had taken her eleven months to repay everything. The man who had destroyed her credit rating and almost destroyed her life was gone. And she had a new job. The new, resolute Molly was ready to build a new life…but one without a man. She might have a terrible address at that moment and no long-term, well-paid career prospects, but she had done the best she could.

Hindsight would have seen her make very different financial decisions. But hindsight was

like that. It was wise and sensible. And she had
been neither when she'd met the man she'd
thought would be her happily ever after. She
had rushed in and believed every word he had
whispered in her ear. Hung on every promise he'd made in the warmth of the bed they'd
shared. Trusted every dream he'd told her as
she'd smiled at her beautiful diamond engagement ring. She'd thought her life was turning
around after the sadness of losing her parents.
She'd believed she had found the one. The man
who would make her dreams come true. The
one who would make her life whole again.

But all of it was a lie. A well-planned, bril-
liantly executed lie.

And one she had willingly and naively
bought into and lost almost everything she had
in the process. But fortunately, not everything.
She still had her most treasured, shining ace.

She had Tommy.

Looking up into the falling raindrops, she
didn't know whether to laugh or cry. And so,
she did neither. Instead she let the water run
over her face, waking her up completely, while
her icy fingers felt around in the bottom of
her bag for her makeshift breakfast. She un-
wrapped it and unceremoniously wolfed it
down in three bites. At least the pain in her
head was subsiding and·while she was quite

powerless to change much about the morning, she could at least prevent her stomach growling with hunger. The very first day of winter was testing her mettle but she would get through it. She had Tommy and together they could face whatever life threw at them. They had already proven that.

Suddenly the thought of her younger brother warmed her heart and went a little way to quelling her rising anxiety. He more than made up for the wreck the other parts of her life had become. And on the days when she felt herself spinning a little close to the edge, knowing they had each other kept her grounded.

And that day would be no different.

Whatever the world threw at her, she would face it head-on.

She had to do that for Tommy.

CHAPTER TWO

'YOU'RE PRETTY.'

Molly lifted her bright blue eyes from the keyboard at the reception desk that had been officially hers for four hours. Her lips instinctively curved upwards to form something close to a smile at the unexpected compliment. It was the last thing she'd expected to hear. Pretty was nowhere close to how she felt. In her mind, bedraggled would have been a more accurate call but she was trying not to think about her appearance and just get on with the job at hand. She was warm and dry and that was an improvement on the start of her day. Grooming had not been a priority that morning but hearing the young woman's compliment definitely lifted her spirits.

'Thank you. I think you're very kind to say something so sweet,' Molly told the young woman who had fronted the desk. 'I think you're very pretty and I love your red boots.'

The young woman, just like Molly's brother, Tommy, had been born with Down's syndrome and just like Tommy, she appeared to be relatively independent, by virtue of her attending the surgery without a caregiver by her side. Molly noticed she was wearing designer jeans and a red jumper under her checked woollen overcoat that also looked as if it had been bought at a high-end store. Her short blonde hair was in a bob style and the flat red ankle boots completed the outfit. She was quite the young fashionista.

'Thank you. Red is my favourite colour in the world.'

'I must agree. Red is lovely,' Molly told her, then continued. 'May I have your name, please?'

'Lizzy Jones,' the young woman said. 'My boyfriend likes red. He didn't like red before he was my boyfriend. Now he likes red.'

Molly smiled at the thought of the young man changing his favourite colour to match his girlfriend's taste. Young love was so sweet and naive and something to be treasured as it rarely stayed that perfect. When the rose-coloured glasses came off the real man was rarely as perfect as he once seemed. She hoped for Lizzy's sake her boyfriend remained as lovely as he was at that moment.

'Do you have a boyfriend?' Lizzy asked, breaking Molly's train of thought.

'Um…no, no, I don't.'

'You should have a boyfriend. It's nice. You can share lunch and hold hands.'

'I will give it some thought,' Molly said politely, all the while thinking quite the opposite. Boyfriends, fiancés, they were all the same. They brought heartbreak and disappointment and she was not going back there. Not ever.

'My dad doesn't know I have a boyfriend.' Lizzy giggled then covered her mouth with her hand. 'I will tell him maybe next week or maybe at Christmas.'

'It's a long time until Christmas,' Molly told her with her eyebrow arched slightly.

'Mmm…maybe next week. I don't know.'

'That might be a good idea to let your father know you have a boyfriend. He might like to meet him. I'm sure he's very nice.'

'Shh,' Lizzy said with her fingers at her lips and looking a little anxious. 'You can't tell when you see him.'

'Don't worry, I won't, I promise,' Molly replied with a smile, wondering if Lizzy's father was parking the car or running late to meet her. Whatever the case she hadn't hesitated to reassure the young woman. She had become visibly agitated and needed reassurance that her secret was safe. Molly could see no purpose in announcing to a complete stranger that his daughter had a boyfriend when it might be nothing more than puppy love. And none of her business.

'Okay,' Lizzy said before she crossed the room and made herself comfortable on a waiting-room chair.

Molly sensed Lizzy was quite at ease with being in the practice, almost as if it were a second home to her. She checked the appointment schedule. Forty-five minutes had been allocated for Lizzy Jones, which was unusual considering the pace of the morning, and there was no reference to patient notes available online. She wasn't listed as a new patient but she wasn't in the records management system either. Molly found all of it unusual and decided she would raise it with Ryan later.

There were no other patients waiting as they had been running early and the previous patient had just left. Molly glanced up periodically and noticed Lizzy had taken off her overcoat and neatly placed it on the chair beside her. She was happily swinging her legs and glancing around at the paintings on the wall. Sometime in the ensuing minutes while Molly was processing correspondence Lizzy made her way back to the reception desk.

'Are your shoes red?' Lizzy asked excitedly.

Molly jumped with the surprise of having the young woman upon her again without warning. Then she cringed at the thought of her mismatched shoes. As a knee-jerk reaction to feeling more than a little self-conscious she placed one foot on top of the other. Quite purposely squashing the solo bow on her left foot.

'Umm…'

Before she had a chance to finish her reply a deep male voice came from somewhere close behind her.

'Well, Lizzy, I'm looking at them now and they're definitely not red. Actually, it would appear that Miss Murphy couldn't quite decide whether to wear blue or black shoes today… so she chose one of each colour and threw in a bow of sorts…but only on one of them.'

'That's funny,' Lizzy said with a wide grin that further lit up her happy face.

'Well, funny's one way to describe it,' the male voice countered. 'Another would be odd. Quite literally.'

Molly didn't turn. She was only too well aware it was her boss of four hours. The far too perfect Dr Ryan McFetridge. Charcoal-eyed, raven-haired, six-foot-two, sole general practitioner to the wealthy and privileged who happened to need a temp office manager at the same time that Molly needed a job, any job. It was her only option to ensure she and Tommy were not evicted by the week's end. And that morning as she had stood in the rain watching the bus pull away a tiny part of her had feared that might happen.

'Do you like to mix it up?' the deep voice continued, bringing Molly back from her unsettling thoughts.

Molly drew a deep breath, plastered on a smile and spun to face her boss. His perfect smile made the picture even more ridiculous. And made her feel even more self-conscious. She was bedraggled and he was standing so close with his leading-man looks, not to mention a voice as smooth as melted chocolate. She knew the type. He had playboy written all over him. But he didn't impress her. Not in the least. Molly Murphy had sworn off men…and nothing was going to sway that vow.

'Or was it a case of dressing in the dark?' he continued as he stepped to the side a little and, opening one of the filing cabinets, began sifting through old hard-copy case notes. After finding what he wanted, he returned his gaze to her but said nothing.

'Actually, you nailed it,' she responded without expression in her voice or on her face.

'I did dress in the dark this morning, quite literally.'

'Power outage?'

'Of sorts,' she replied, not liking the fact he hadn't broken eye contact. For some unknown reason, despite her showing no emotion, he was unsettling her. It wasn't his line of questioning. It was his proximity to her. Through his clothes and her own, she could almost sense the warmth of his body. It was as if her own body was adjusting its thermostat to his and she was enormously relieved when he stepped away.

'That would explain a lot.'

Molly wasn't sure what the comment alluded to but assumed it was her previously wet hair and clothes. Before she could take him to task on the meaning behind his remark, he popped the patient record under his arm and then asked Lizzy to follow him to the consulting room.

As the two of them disappeared, Molly was angry with herself. Why the hell was she reacting to him being so close? She should be angry with him but instead she felt a warm wave wash over her and suspected her cheeks might be flushed. She was appalled and surprised.

Molly had met Ryan briefly when she had first arrived, flustered and rushed. She accepted he was an extremely good-looking man but their meeting had been brief, and from a distance across the office as he'd taken an early arriving patient into his consulting room. She had been more interested in settling into the job with the assistance of the young nurse, Stacy, who was there arranging influenza shots and bloods. Molly just wanted to stay under the radar and unnoticed herself, rather than noticing too much about her employer. But suddenly, now, she had noticed far too much about him.

The handsome medico was dressed straight from a men's designer store, the kind of store filled with expensive leather shoes and every imported suit hanging an equal distance from the next on the rack, all covered with shoulder protectors, and assorted silk ties dressing shirts that were housed in open mahogany display cabinets. She knew the stores only too well. A year before, she and her fiancé had been regular customers of them. Her fiancé was quite the clothes horse and she had unwittingly been footing the bill. Ever since, the stores and the people who shopped there had held no appeal to her.

And there was Dr McFetridge's elegantly decorated consulting rooms in one of Adelaide's most affluent eastern suburbs. The leafy side streets were lined with large, opulent, double-storey homes with return driveways and at least three imported cars while Molly's home had no driveway, which was fine as she had no car to park in one anyway. She had sold it along with her jewellery to cover the bond on her home and buy some simple furnishings. And she could get by just fine without it. Except for this morning, when a car would have been very handy.

Everything about Ryan was impeccable. She assumed his designer underwear would match his socks too. Black and more than likely the finest imported woven silk…

She stopped mid-thought and shook herself mentally. What had got into her? And why on earth was she even thinking about her employer's underwear? It had to have been the knock to her head. Or perhaps being celibate for a year was affecting her reasoning, she decided. But it hadn't until that moment. The need to have a man in her life was below the need to match the colour of the bin liner to the trash can. Of no importance and not worth a second thought. And a man like Dr McFetridge was not on her wish list; no man was.

Perhaps it was the significance of the day that was making her react. That had to be it, she told herself, and the next day would be different. She wouldn't be having the melancholy thoughts and she wouldn't give her boss even a second thought.

But she begrudgingly admitted to herself that she did like his cologne. The fresh woody fragrance was still lingering. Fragrance had not been her priority that morning. She was lucky to get close to soap and nothing about her lingerie matched. Molly's stomach dropped and she moved in her seat to confirm in her rush she had remembered underwear. She breathed a sigh of relief when she could feel the elastic of her knickers. Thankfully she had grabbed one of the three pairs pegged to a coat hanger to dry over the bath the night before. She cringed momentarily.

If they had not been hanging in her line of sight would she be wearing any?

Just as quickly yet another unsettling thought swept into her mind. She pushed it aside. They were on and she didn't need to dwell on what might or might not have been. It had been a ridiculously rushed start to her first day but with a smidgen of Irish luck, from her father's side, she had made it with five minutes to spare. Although after seeing the consulting rooms she wondered just how long he would keep her on staff. It was only too obvious to Molly that appearance certainly counted with him. His dress sense, his rooms, all of it was immaculate.

And she was not. Well, not at that time. She had previously dressed well and taken pride in her hair and make-up, but equal amounts of money and sleep deprivation meant both had gone to pot. And nothing much about that was going to change overnight. But she was clean and efficient. Like the pitch to sell a small imported car, she thought.

Her mind was jumbled and she had to stay focussed. It couldn't be that difficult. He was just another tall, dark, good-looking man and she was not interested in men, tall, short, dark or fair; she was not interested in being used and lied to again. And stripped of her faith in humanity…and her worldly possessions…in one fell swoop.

She opened her eyes just as quickly and, looking around at everything, she was reminded that, while she no doubt looked out of place in Ryan McFetridge's practice, her skills should ensure she stayed put as long as possible and enable her to meet the rent and avoid Joel's advances.

Despite her decision not to bite back too fiercely, Molly could not roll over and let another man think his looks would allow him to act in a way that was just wrong in her book.

While it was only her shoes, she had to put a line in the sand and retain a little dignity. She had made it to work on time and he had no idea what she had been through to get there. So what if her shoes didn't match? As if it mattered in the scheme of things—her feet were hidden behind the desk and it didn't make her less competent, she reminded herself, all the while feeling quite ridiculous and uncomfortably exposed. Although she did not truly feel the level of bravado she was trying to exude, she would do her best to let her temporary employer know where she stood.

Twenty minutes later, Lizzy and Ryan reappeared. He placed the notes on the reception desk, and Molly couldn't help but notice he patted the dog-eared records almost affectionately. She was even more confused.

'I'll need you to make another time for Lizzy in four weeks with Dr Slattery. His details are on the notes here. And can you make it a time that I can attend with her so block out ninety minutes in my calendar too, please, Molly, to allow for my travel time.'

'Certainly,' Molly replied, then, wondering why Ryan would be accompanying his patient to see another medico, added, 'Is this for a second opinion?'

'No, it's not a second opinion. Lizzy is Dr Slattery's patient.'

'Okay, I'll call his rooms and make that time now.'

Molly didn't quite understand but decided not to question him further. However, she did need to address something. His remarks about her shoes were playing on her mind. She wanted to be clear in what she would tolerate and what she wouldn't and wanted to address it before Ryan disappeared back into his room.

'I'll make the time right away, then after that I could take a lunch break, go home and collect matching shoes if you think they're an issue.' Molly's tone was not confronting but it was firm and resolute. She was respectful of Lizzy's presence and aware she was witnessing everything.

There was silence for a moment. Molly watched as Ryan's eyebrow raised but she quickly sensed amusement rather than annoyance in his expression. It was almost as if his eyes were saying *'bravo to you'* but his lips hadn't moved, not even twitched.

She was incredibly confused and that had not happened to her in a very long time. For the last year she had felt confident that she could size up a man quickly. There were two categories: not to be trusted and those over sixty-five.

'That won't be necessary,' he told her. 'You look perfectly fine just as you are.'

Molly was taken aback by his response but didn't have time to say anything as he continued.

'Lizzy, I don't think you've met Molly. She's my new office manager and she'll be here for the next month. You'll see her whenever you call in to visit me.' Ryan paused again for a moment, his eyes darting between the two women, as if deep in thought. Then he continued, 'Molly, I'd like you to meet my daughter, Elizabeth, who prefers to be called Lizzy, and the aforementioned red shoes are her favourite.'

Molly almost fell off her seat. She had not seen that coming at all. Dr McPerfect had a teenage daughter. She suddenly understood why Ryan wanted to attend her appointment with her general practitioner and why Lizzy wasn't on the record management system. Lizzy was his daughter, not his patient, despite having a different surname. And if Molly had heard correctly, he wanted her to stay on for the length of the assignment. He apparently wasn't about to fire her for rushing in at the last minute looking as if she had been plucked from a downpipe.

Ryan was not the man she had imagined at all.

Watching the way Ryan walked from behind the reception desk and over to Lizzy, putting his arm around her in such a loving way, made Molly's heart soften just a little. Suddenly Molly saw him as just Lizzy's father, although he didn't look old enough to have a daughter Lizzy's age. She felt her heart almost skip a beat. There was something in the way his dark eyes smiled as he pulled his daughter protectively to him that to her surprise took Molly's breath away. It was an unconditional love he had for her. And she knew that feeling so very well. It was exactly how she felt when Tommy gave her a hug goodnight. And it was the feeling that kept her going when everything else in her life was turning to mud.

Molly had thought she had men safely locked away. They were not to be trusted. Period. Suddenly Ryan was testing her bias. Suddenly she realised that she had been the one casting judgement on her boss because she was afraid of being judged. Dr McFetridge was keeping her on staff even though she had assumed she did not fit his vision of perfect. Perhaps it was her idea of what perfect should look like that was skewing her outlook. Everything about the previous five minutes had taken her aback. She had been the one guilty of assuming the book was the total of the cover.

Molly was quickly being forced to accept that perhaps there might actually be more to Dr McFetridge than handsome packaging.

CHAPTER THREE

RYAN HAD WANTED uninterrupted father-daughter time to discuss the medical issues at hand and then link via a telephone conference to discuss the prognosis and potential treatment plan with Lizzy's GP and the specialist.

A choice would need to be made but Ryan had no intention of rushing into a decision that didn't sit well with his daughter. He had removed his own GP hat and had worn his father hat during the conversation. There were a number of considerations moving forward. How his daughter felt about each and every one of them was paramount to Ryan. With the options clearly explained, Ryan wanted to sit and talk more with Lizzy before making their joint decision and visiting her doctor.

Finally, a driver arrived to collect her. Ryan waved goodbye and walked his next patient into his consulting room and closed the door.

He sat down opposite the older woman and leaned in towards her slightly.

'Tell me, Dorothy, how are you and how is the adjusted medication level coming along?'

'Not too bad, Doctor.'

The elderly lady's reply didn't convince Ryan as he watched as her softly wrinkled hands fidgeted with her handkerchief. She was twisting the delicate lace-edged linen nervously.

'Not too bad?' he replied. 'That's not what I was hoping to hear and it's not the same as good. I would like to hear that you're feeling very well, Dorothy. You're the most energetic and engaging octogenarian I know. What's bothering you?'

He didn't take his eyes away from hers. Ryan was not going to let her leave without an explanation.

'Well.' She paused for a moment then took a considered breath and continued. 'My sugar readings are all around six or seven, which you told me is fine, but the headaches are still there. Every day I have one. Some days I even wake up with one and, on those days, they are particularly bad. I don't like taking painkillers but George says I must take them or I'm like a grumpy bear. He makes sure I do every four hours and gets quite cross if I don't want to take them. I don't want to upset him and I would hate to be a grumpy bear but I'm taking twelve of those tablets a day and that can't be good.'

Ryan's displeasure with George's behaviour towards his wife, insisting that she take the tablets rather than solving the problem, showed in his frown. 'George is not qualified, Dorothy. And you should not need that level of medication, so let's get to the reason for the headaches.'

He did not further push his annoyance that George was encouraging the painkillers without consultation with a professional. Dorothy Dunstan, in Ryan's opinion, was as far from a grumpy bear as one could get. Even in pain. The eighty-one-year-old was a slightly built woman, with a mass of white curls, stunning blue eyes and the sweetest smile. He had no doubt she would have been very beautiful as a younger woman and her prettiness would more than likely still turn heads in the upmarket retirement village where the couple lived.

Her husband, George, on the other hand, also a patient of Ryan's practice, was a solidly built man with a gruff demeanour and very much closer to a bear's disposition on the best of days, particularly when his diverticulosis flared up and he blamed everyone around him.

Ryan was upset that the man would force his wife to take medication just to keep her happy around him.

'Let's trial a break of your current medication. That may help with the headaches. No guarantee but it's worth trying that route.'

'Really, Doctor? But what about my diabetes?'

'The surgery to remove your gall bladder last November also removed the chronic infection. That would have been stressing your body and as a result a number of organs were not functioning properly and your blood sugar level became elevated. I have been lowering your dose each month, as you know, but now I would like you to stop taking your medication completely for one week.' Ryan paused and looked Dorothy in the eyes with a serious expression dressing his face. 'But, Dorothy, you must maintain a diet without any added sugar as the dietician advised. None. No chocolates or other sugary treats. That means no cakes or biscuits with your cup of tea…and no scones, jam and cream either.'

'I promise, Dr McFetridge, but I do love Devonshire teas and it has been very hard to say no to my friends when they make scones. And George buys us both cake with our coffee after lawn bowls and I don't like to say no to him.'

George's selfish and ignorant attitude was testing Ryan's patience but he controlled his desire to tell Dorothy what he thought of her husband. 'I know, but you also want to stay healthy and drug free so it's worth the sacrifice and I'm sure that your friends and George love you enough to understand. But you must tell them and you must be firm.'

Dorothy nodded in response.

'And I want you to call through your blood sugar reading every day to my nurse. Any raised levels and I need to see you straight away. Don't try to persevere if the levels change. I can't reiterate this enough. Diabetes is a serious condition, but as it only occurred after your illness we may be able to control it with a sensible diet from here on in. But it will mean ongoing monitoring and food restrictions.'

'Really? You mean I may not need to take the medication again, ever?'

'Let's hope so. In some cases, an adjusted diet is all the treatment a patient needs and I hope you are one of the fortunate ones. Would you like me to tell George that he should refrain from buying the cake and the painkillers?'

'Oh, Lord, no. He would have a fit if he

thought I'd told you that.' Dorothy's disposition was suddenly flustered.

'You can rest assured that I won't say anything, then, Dorothy, but you need to be firm with him. And I do mean firm. You can't eat the cakes just because your husband has bought one for each of you.'

'I'll just tell him I'm not hungry.'

'You can tell George whatever you like, that is not my business, although I would have thought telling him the truth about your condition would be better, but again that's not my place to advise you how best to manage George. However...' He paused and his voice became increasingly deep and more serious in tone. 'Whatever you tell him, you must not waver under pressure. It's your long-term health that we are talking about here. And George would most definitely want a healthy wife.'

She nodded her agreement to Ryan's terms then continued. 'If I stop the medication and avoid the temptation of the sweets, do you think my headache will finally go away?'

'That's what I'm hoping,' Ryan told her as he stood.

'Then that's wonderful news and worth the sacrifice of a few cakes...'

'*All* cakes, not a few cakes.'

'That's what I meant.'

Ryan smiled as he reached for Dorothy's arm and lifted her to her feet and walked her out to the reception area, asking Molly to make an appointment for the following week.

He left Dorothy with Molly, then turned and smiled in her husband's direction. 'How are you today, George? Keeping dry and out of the cold as much as you can, I hope.'

George grunted and made a dismissive gesture with his hand. 'Damned appointments all day. After this I have to go home, pick up Dorothy's darned cat and get her to the vet. Furballs again. If it's not one thing it's another. So much for retirement. I never get a day at home in peace. And the cat doesn't like me anyway. It either hisses at me or ignores me. Typical woman.'

Ryan wasn't sure quite what to say. The elderly man was healthy for his age, with relatively few ailments, but his demeanour was another story. He behaved as if he had the weight of the world on his shoulders, and nothing appeared to make him happy. Ryan had initially suspected a level of depression but that was quickly ruled out by a referral to a clinical psychologist. George had retired from his successful fishing charter business in the lower Eyre Peninsula town of Port Lincoln a very wealthy man. He had a very sweet wife, the two of them had taken numerous extended overseas holidays and were active for their age, and their four daughters had provided them with half a dozen healthy, happy grandchildren. If only, Ryan thought, there were a medication to remedy a glass-half-empty outlook on life. George's cup was chipped, stained and the handle missing most days and he truly had no idea how fortunate he was to have the love and devotion of a woman as wonderful as Dorothy for over sixty years.

Ryan knew that he would never have that same unconditional love and, in his heart, he knew why. He would never trust anyone to get that close to him again.

Ryan walked back into his office leaving Dorothy Dunstan speaking with Molly. He hoped that she had listened to his instructions and would adhere to the strict diet, and the headaches would in time subside. There was of course a very good chance that the cause of her daily headache was George, and if that was the case there really was no medicinal cure. The only cure would be to leave him. And a woman like Dorothy would never consider that an option.

As he closed his door, Ryan's thoughts unexpectedly turned from Dorothy to Molly. Molly, with her uncontrolled mop of brown curls and contagious smile. And feisty attitude. The agency had told him Molly Murphy would be temping at the office to replace Maxine, his office manager of six years who had slipped and broken her arm in her Zumba class. Immediately he had formed a picture in his mind of a pleasant and efficient Irish woman in her late fifties or early sixties to replace his very efficient but now injured gym junkie and almost sixty-year-old office manager. With an image of the Irish replacement having a love of home knits, wonderful cooking skills and a slight brogue accent, Ryan felt confident the woman would meet the needs of the family-focussed practice for four weeks. She would be the wholesome motherly figure like Maxine whom his patients would like and adapt to quickly.

Then Molly had arrived and she didn't come close to his vision. In her mid to late twenties, she had no Irish accent, and she didn't seem the type to sit home knitting. She had shot his clichéd assumptions out of the water. She certainly was a conundrum. And more than a little difficult to read. He had observed her open and comforting rapport with patients during the morning and decided that her chosen path in a medical support role matched her natural affinity with people and his patients would quickly warm to her, but there was something that didn't add up. Her administration skills appeared more than competent but her medical expertise appeared more aligned to that of a doctor or nurse. He had overheard her speaking to more than one patient and the level of detail she provided exposed the true depth of her knowledge. The agency had not provided a résumé as his request had come at short notice but Molly came highly recommended and very quickly Ryan could see why.

He couldn't deny he was curious about her. There was definitely more to Molly Murphy than met the eye.

At odds with her empathetic nature was a woman who had come out fighting like a cornered alley cat when he'd mentioned her dubious footwear. He was grateful that he hadn't raised the matter of her arriving drenched to the bone with only minutes to spare.

He shook his head a little as he crossed to his desk and opened up the emails on his computer. Not many people surprised Ryan McFetridge any more. He treated most people with a level of distrust until they could prove otherwise and he believed that he could fairly easily and accurately sum them up. But he didn't feel

his usual level of confidence about his sum-
mation of Molly. He wasn't sure what he felt
but it did unsettle him that he felt something.

He closed his emails. There was nothing of
interest, just a reminder about a medical association event he had agreed to attend the next
evening and some pharmaceutical promotions.
Running one hand through his short black hair,
he opened the afternoon patient roster as he
routinely did after every morning's appointments were completed. He did a double take
and, far from being annoyed, his interest was
piqued when he saw changes to the layout of
the next day's patient listing. He hovered the
cursor over the first name and the medical history and purpose of the appointment appeared.
He tried it again on the next patient and again
the function allowed him access to the notes
of the previous three visits without going into
each patient's records. It was an abbreviated
medical history with a link to archived notes.
He smirked. Molly Murphy had been doing
some upgrades. The reference to these details
was an impressive feature and a function of the
software package that he had never accessed
because he hadn't been aware it existed. Molly
certainly knew the program well. And Ryan
was more than impressed. He had not asked
for improvements, nor had the busy schedule

provided her with additional time on her hands to do this out of boredom. Molly had used initiative to make improvements. Again, she had surprised him and that never happened. Not any more.

Molly Murphy, he thought, you might just be the perfect for-ever woman...*for my practice*, he quickly qualified.

Ryan McFetridge had no need for a forever woman in any other area of his life. And particularly not a woman like Molly. She appeared very different from the women with whom Ryan kept company. Her manner with patients was genuine. The empathy showed a warm heart beneath her shapeless clothes. The women Ryan preferred wore clothes that hugged their shapes but underneath there was no sign of a heart. And that suited him. A night of mutual satisfaction with a woman who was not wanting or expecting more was all he wanted.

Because Ryan McFetridge had nothing to give. Nor did he want anything back.

He rested back in his large black leather chair, a touch of melancholy colouring his mood as he swivelled to look out through the rain-spotted window to the overcast streetscape. It was cold and miserable, with few people in sight, but for some inexplicable reason Ryan felt different. His mood was lighter. And Ryan had not felt anything close to that in a very long time. He brushed aside the coincidence of his mood lifting on the same day that Molly had started work. It was just that. A coincidence. It couldn't be anything more.

His sole focus outside his work was his daughter. She was his motivation to keep going. To build a legacy to ensure she never needed or wanted for anything. That responsibility weighed heavily. And he would never let her down.

Or ever let anyone hurt her.

Ever again.

Swivelling back on his chair and returning his focus to his computer screen, he realised Molly Murphy knew her stuff and he couldn't help but wonder about her background and her qualifications. And why she was working in a role that Ryan suspected was far less than her capability. He knew so little about her. He had to admit to himself he had noticed she was not wearing a wedding ring. He didn't know why he'd even looked. But with Molly he was curious to know more. Although the absence didn't mean there was no significant other in her life. And he reminded himself that she could potentially have children, although they would be relatively young.

But none of it mattered, he continued to remind himself. She was his office manager. Nothing more. Nothing less. But it still didn't stop thoughts of her occupying his head. She was pretty in an almost fragile way but she had spunk and clearly knew how to take care of herself. And now his practice. There was something about Molly that reminded Ryan of the weather outside...unpredictable and challenging.

And Ryan McFetridge had always loved winter.

He drummed his fingers on the edge of his mahogany desk. It was inlaid with a deep burgundy leather and not in keeping with the rest of the more modern decor but it had been a graduation gift from his parents. As they had both since died not long after he'd opened his practice in Adelaide, he loved having something to remind him of them every day. His childhood had been happy and filled with love and encouragement and one of Ryan's many regrets was that Lizzy had never met her paternal grandparents.

He rested his chin on one hand as he began to scan through his emails. He needed to get back on track and stop being distracted by random thoughts, especially those of his new staff member. Pondering the unknown was pointless and wasting time. He reminded himself firmly that Molly Murphy's past, present or future after the immediate four-week placement was not his business. With common sense born from the realities he had faced over the years since Lizzy had come into his life, Ryan knew, no matter what effect Molly was or wasn't having on him, he had to keep it purely business.

Despite her best intentions, Molly's own curiosity continued to niggle at her new-found peace of mind. Lingering doubts were replaced by an unsettling and growing interest in knowing a little more about her temporary boss. As much as she also tried to push thoughts about Ryan away as she sipped on lunch, they kept returning. While she felt secure in the knowledge that she had ongoing employment for a month, she felt concerned about why she wanted to know more about her employer. And his daughter. She wondered if Lizzy was using her mother's surname or maiden name. Not that any of it mattered. She was not naturally curious but now, for some inexplicable reason, she wanted to know more than was necessary to carry out her job.

Why did he have to be so damned attractive and, from all appearances, a loving father? she thought as she pursed her lips. She gently blew on her spoonful of soup in an attempt to cool it slightly. She had not been interested in men since her engagement ended. And she had to keep it that way. He was a man giving her employment for a month. And in her financial situation it was not unlike a rope to a drowning man. A godsend. She couldn't confuse gratitude for anything more than that. She couldn't afford to romanticise the situation.

Molly felt sure that she had reconciled the situation in her head and definitely quelled any thoughts stirring in her heart. It was relief and gratitude turning her emotions upside down. Nothing more, she decided as she continued eating her lunch, glancing occasionally out through the rain-splattered window. The weather was still dismal and, on top of the rain, she had discovered when she'd dashed out to find lunch that the bitterly cold breeze had not abated. A patient had told her that falling branches and trees had knocked down power lines in the foothills. It was only slightly better in their location as a powerful gust blowing down the street cut through her thick coat during her mad dash out, once again chilling her to the bone. An arctic freeze, one patient remarked.

She was grateful she had taken the earlier dampness out of her hair with the hand-dryer in the restroom and borrowed an umbrella from Stacy or she might have brought the stirrings of a winter head cold back to the practice with her. But climate aside, Molly's day had insurmountably improved from the rocky start. A month's employment was everything she needed at that moment. She knew rent would be covered and she could save a little for unexpected bills. Finally, she could exhale if only for a few weeks and that brought her great comfort. As did her warm surroundings that she studied in a little more detail.

The lunchroom was brightly lit, with a round white wooden table and four matching chairs with red cushions and an arrangement of fresh red and yellow gerberas, which she knew must have been imported at that time of the year; a well-stocked wall-mounted magazine rack that was female friendly in choices; and the usual kitchen amenities, including a red enamelled espresso machine and red mugs. Molly had wondered if Lizzy might have had input into arranging the pretty room since there were many not so subtle splashes of red in the decor.

A few moments later Ryan made his way into the lunchroom, slightly startling Molly. She had assumed he had left the practice for

his home rounds. There were five visits that
afternoon and Molly discovered Ryan, unlike
many GPs, didn't use a locum service to meet
his patients' needs. He called in personally to
monitor those who were housebound by various short- and long-term medical ailments,
including those patients who had been admitted permanently to nursing homes. He seemed
more like a country-style, hands-on GP.

'Molly,' Ryan said as he made his way to the
refrigerator and collected milk. 'I wondered if
you might be in here.'

'Just grabbing a bite to eat.'

'Ah, soup,' he said, peering into the bowl as
he passed by. 'Is it home-made?'

'No, the local shop,' she mumbled as she
swallowed and pointed in the direction of the
local bakery across the road. 'I didn't have
time to think about breakfast this morning, let
alone packing lunch.'

Ryan smiled in reply and made his way
to the espresso machine. 'I'm not much of a
breakfast person, slice of toast on the way out
of the door if I'm lucky, but I never go without
my coffee. I'm addicted to caffeine, I can't lie.'

'It's not a serious vice,' she returned, happy
their conversation was light and casual and he
was on the other side of the room. Her emotions were in check and he was just a hand-

some doctor making chit-chat. It was easy, she told herself. She had clearly overreacted before to being in a new environment.

'I agree, there's worse,' he said as he turned his back on the machine and faced Molly with his arms folded across his chest. 'Before I head off for the afternoon, I wanted to say thank you for the changes that you made to the scheduling.'

'You're welcome. I like the software and you hadn't been utilising all of the features.'

'It's great. I had no idea the software had that capability.'

'I've seen it at a number of practices, and even some small country hospitals use it. The bigger ones not so much.'

'So, you've done some country placements in admin too, then?'

'As a nurse, I accessed the software for patient notes and was impressed so I looked into it further.' As the words slipped from her lips she realised she had said more than she intended. 'Keep it simple and short' had been her plan. Since the break-up Molly just wanted to keep her life a closed book. Information to be provided on an as-needed basis. But again, she felt safe. Ryan was just her boss and things were professional and she didn't need to worry.

Ryan swung around to collect his coffee,

then back to Molly. 'Nursing background? Now it makes sense.' He nodded to himself. 'I heard you speaking earlier to a patient, Jean Burton, and the level of detail in answering her questions about her blood-pressure medication was so much more information than an admin assistant or receptionist would, or for that matter generally could, provide.'

'You haven't seen my CV, then?'

'No. The agency told me you were highly recommended but no in-depth details. To be honest I didn't have the time to look through CVs last week. With Maxine's accident I just needed a replacement asap so I had to trust them…and I'm glad I did,' Ryan said as he pulled up a seat and put his freshly made coffee on the table before him. His long, lean fingers were comfortably wrapped around the hot mug.

It was at complete odds with how uncomfortable Molly was suddenly made by his decision to sit down with her. Everything she had told herself about him having no effect on her was being negated quickly.

'Are you a registered nurse?'

'I'm… I'm actually an anaesthetic nurse.'

'Any reason you specialised in anaesthesia?'

'I did a Theatre placement during my second year and realised that was where I wanted to be after graduating, so that's what I did.'

He sat back in his seat, releasing his hands from the cup. 'Then you are a very long way from home, Dorothy.'

His smile was wide and Molly sensed genuine. But it was also making her pulse pick up speed. She had to get it under control. She wasn't sure how but she suspected distance might help.

'Not so far, really,' she said matter-of-factly. 'I'm still working in the field of medicine...'

'You are and, believe me, I'm not complaining,' he cut in as he once again leaned forward.

To Molly's horror he made the distance between them even less. His forest-fresh cologne brought a sudden tingling sensation to her skin.

'Your medical experience is a huge benefit to my practice, but may I ask why you stepped away from Theatre?'

'Long story and I won't bore you. Just say that the temp hours suit me better.'

'I shouldn't imagine the remuneration would so much,' he said matter-of-factly with a frown forming, replacing the previous light-hearted expression. 'I suppose we stand a chance of losing you, then. I mean, if a better-paid gig came along in line with your experience, with the hours you want, then I couldn't, and I wouldn't, blame you for leaving.'

'You don't have to worry about that happening,' she said, hoping her racing heart wasn't making her blush. 'If I make a promise or commitment I always keep it. This suits me just fine.'

'In the interim perhaps, but long-term maybe not so much—'

'Let's not fudge words,' Molly cut in, wanting to end the conversation. 'I'm barely dry after four hours and my typing speed is twenty-nine words a minute. The average for a temp is over eighty. My strength is my medical background and you're offering good hours. So, if you're happy, I'm happy. It's a great trade-off for both of us.'

'I think you're selling yourself short. While I have to agree you arrived a little soggy—I couldn't help but overhear the hand-dryer running for ten minutes straight earlier on,' he told her as he leant back on the chair, his long legs stretched out in front of him, giving her the space she suddenly realised she needed. 'But I need more than a great typist in this practice and I think you'll fit in extremely well. I'm astute enough to see what you've accomplished in a couple of hours. You've made changes I didn't know were possible.'

'It's hardly rocket science but I'm happy you like what I've done. I've been here four hours so it wasn't too difficult to make the changes. You had the software capability, it just needed to be utilised,' Molly answered as she stood up. She had to create the space between them herself so she collected her bowl and cup, and made her way to the sink. She rolled her eyes at the way she had reacted having him so close. She dropped her bowl into the sudsy water in the sink. The unexpected effect he was having on her was absurd…and disconcerting. She wasn't about to be swept off her feet. It was ridiculous. And risky. She had more to lose than gain by thinking that way about a man, let alone her boss, and she would never take a risk again.

'Whether it's been four hours or four weeks, you instinctively searched for ways to make improvements. It was like a four-hour quality-improvement audit. I never asked you to do that and no previous office manager has, no matter how long they were with me. But it was exactly what I needed. You, Molly Murphy, are exactly what I need and I would like to make it worth your while. In fact… I have a proposition for you.'

CHAPTER FOUR

A PROPOSITION?

Molly's eyes darted about as she repeated the words in her head. What on earth could he be talking about? She felt quite sure it wasn't the type of proposition that her body might be silently willing, if he got too close again.

It had to be business, but what? She had a job for a month. Once Maxine's cast came off she'd return to work and Molly would leave. The practice was busy but not enough to warrant two in administration.

She turned around knowing she wore a curious look but she couldn't hide it. His expression appeared serious and, damn, it made him look even more handsome. He was making her question so much about him and herself and it didn't make sense. She was becoming even more unsettled and didn't trust her reaction so she turned back to the sink. Grabbing for the sponge, she washed her cup and her bowl before she rinsed them both and placed them in the otherwise empty dish drainer. She needed something else to keep her busy and delay her turning back to him. Reaching into the warm shallows of the sink, she searched under the bubbles with her fingers for her spoon. Finding it quickly, she washed it thoroughly and rinsed it with the same attention before she put it in the drainer with the other things. Unfortunately, there was nothing else to wash and nothing else to do. There was effectively no way to stall.

She had no choice but to turn back around to the man who was stirring emotions she forgot she could feel. And those she never wanted to feel again. Hoping the feeling was fleeting and born from a mix of her initial job insecurity and gratitude to be in the role for a few weeks, Molly had hoped it would disappear as quickly as it had appeared. But looking at Ryan she knew it hadn't gone or even dampened. It was still there. It felt a little like butterflies…and a lot like…she wasn't sure. But she was confused. It didn't make sense. She barely knew the man and she had sworn herself to a life without one. Men, particularly handsome, confident men like Ryan, brought only trouble into her life and she didn't need any more. She also knew how bedraggled she appeared but for some reason the way he looked at her at that moment made her feel unexpectedly beautiful.

She quickly decided her mind was playing tricks on her. How could she possibly see something in Ryan other than as her boss within a matter of hours of meeting? That didn't happen in real life. That was the stuff of movies. He and she were so very different. He was clearly established and on track with his life, and hers had derailed and she wasn't sure when or even if it would ever truly be travelling in the right direction. Thanks to the man who she had planned to marry.

And she didn't need to have her heart broken again.

Once was more than enough.

She noticed his jaw flick as his eyes slowly pulled away from hers. She sensed he hadn't wanted to look away and that made her confusion grow and those damned butterflies in her stomach flutter manically. It was more than ridiculous. He was her employer, for goodness' sake. Molly had noticed the absence of a wedding ring although she didn't know why she'd registered that fact. She no longer cared about a man's marital status. They were all off-limits in her mind. She couldn't go there. She couldn't let her feelings get the better of her. There was only room in her life for one man and that was Tommy. He had to be her sole focus. No one would ever get close enough to ruin their lives again. Her mind was racing and she appeared to have no control over her thought process.

Without warning, and with purposeful steps, he moved closer to the exit.

'Molly, I can see you're preoccupied, and I've got to get to my home visits, but I want to let you know that I'm proposing a thirty per cent pay increase immediately, I'll call the agency from my car and let them know. And they're not getting a cent of it—it's all yours. You earned it and I hope that might keep you on board and not headhunted. I think you could make a real difference here. If I have anything to do with it, and if I can stop you from getting bored, you might just be with me long after this assignment.'

With that Molly watched Ryan walk from the kitchen as relief and confusion washed over her in waves. Huge waves.

While the logical side of her brain was happy, in fact over the moon, with the pay rise and the idea that the job could be ongoing, her heart, for some crazy, unexplained reason, was even more elated by the prospect of being with him long after the assignment.

Her emotions could not have been more

jumbled at that moment. And she had no control and that worried her. Hadn't she learnt her lesson? She had been resolute in her determination to keep men at arm's length and out of her life and suddenly she was overjoyed by both aspects of his *proposal*.

It was a mix of stupid and ludicrous in equal amounts, and she knew it, but, no matter what her logic and reasoning were reminding her, her heart was definitely beating a little faster than normal and her tummy was doing gentle somersaults. Romantic nonsense. It had to be from the excitement due to the pay rise, the security of a long-term job. Whatever it was, it was immaterial. She had to get a grip and ignore the happiness that was growing inside. She had to think logically. Her clothes were dry and she had a job that could potentially go far longer than the month. Tommy was settled in his job and they had a roof over their heads. She didn't need anything else.

And she didn't want anything else.

She had an outcome to the day she could never have imagined from the soggy start. Brushing the crumbs of bread roll from her skirt, she gathered her wandering thoughts hurriedly as she made her way back to the desk. Ryan had just given her a thirty per cent pay increase so she would forget the sausages and mashed potato she had planned. Molly would be buying Tommy's favourite fish for dinner that night, and if the long-term position was realised then she could potentially look for a new home for the two of them. Goodbye Joel and his advances and the derelict accommodation that she and Tommy had been forced to call home.

If she could just get her heart to slow down and the butterflies to leave, her life would be close to perfect.

Tommy was dropped home fifteen minutes after Molly had raced from the bus stop in the drizzling rain. She'd had enough time to change into her comfortable stretch jeans and a thick baby pink sweater and dry her hair, which had been rained on again on the way home, before she heard her brother putting his key in the door.

Tommy's job didn't pay much at all but it made him happy and that was more than enough for Molly. He couldn't wait to get to work every day and was at the front door early, dressed in one of his two pairs of favourite jeans, a brightly coloured shirt, and in the colder weather he would add a sweater and jacket. He also wore an expectant smile. He liked routine so every day into his backpack he placed a lunch box in which he'd packed a sandwich and a piece of fruit the night before, and which he'd put into the refrigerator. Each morning the bus arrived promptly at seven forty-five, filled with his equally excited friends and work colleagues. Molly and Tommy's house was the last pick-up before the driver finished his round and headed to the workplace with his eager fellow passengers.

Molly had noticed over the previous few weeks that Tommy was beaming a little more than usual as he waited by the door. He spent just a few extra minutes combing his hair and always checked he didn't have his breakfast down the front of his shirt or his trousers. She suspected that as he grew older, Tommy wanted to do his best to be independent. She was so proud of everything he managed on a daily basis and she encouraged him to try new tasks. Each one he accomplished brought him added confidence.

During the previous four weeks, his demeanour had been a mix of excitement and nervousness as he'd waited and she hadn't been completely sure she understood why. But had decided not to ask. As long as he was happy and looking forward to each day, then Molly was happy too. Whatever the impetus for his new-found joy, she knew in time he would tell her. Her baby brother had something in his life that made him feel a level of happiness that Molly had been scared he would never feel again when they had lost their home.

That morning she hadn't heard the driver beep his horn to let Tommy know they were waiting outside, nor had she heard his deep voice calling out to her to say goodbye. Not even the front door being slammed closed as Tommy had run to the gate had disturbed her. He must have been so excited to get on the bus that he'd forgotten to hug her goodbye. He had been a man on a mission.

And Molly had slept through all of it. The worry of finances had kept her counting bills, not sheep, into the early hours. It was a worry she couldn't halve by sharing it with him. His happy disposition didn't need to be brought down by seeing her concerned so Molly kept a brave face until he was in bed.

He had told her he was saving his money to buy a ring and a house when he found a pretty girl to marry. Then he'd changed his mind and said they could all live together because he didn't want his sister to be alone. Molly hadn't been entirely sure when or if her younger brother would find the right girl to fill or appreciate a heart as big as his, but loved the fact he had included her in his plans. He was the sweetest brother a girl could ever hope to have and she felt blessed every day.

She had signed up to a temp agency knowing it would assist in the short-term. The long-term prospects were potentially dire if she couldn't return to her nursing, but the long shifts were close to impossible to manage in her current situation. At least now, with the pay rise, for the time being she could relax. Her life that had been wound very tightly had now slightly loosened.

Leaving Tommy to arrive home to an empty house, cook and eat alone at night had not been an option so she had chosen a lower-paid role to ensure she was home when his bus pulled up each night. After dinner, he would happily watch television with her or sometimes he would go to his room and watch one of his favourite shows in bed.

The remuneration as an office manager up to now hadn't been close to that of an anaesthetic nurse with Molly's skills, but it had meant she wouldn't be caught up in Theatre in a longer than expected operation and not be able to be there for Tommy. The stress of that occurring was too much for her to deal with on a daily basis.

'How was work today, Tommy?' Molly asked as she plated their special dinner of grilled

salmon and steamed vegetables courtesy of
Ryan's generous offer.

'Good,' he told her as he tucked his napkin into the belt of his trousers and sat waiting at the table for two in their small but clean
home. The structure was old and worn but the
atmosphere was always happy. The table was
set with a pretty floral tablecloth, two glasses
of water and a small basket with some sliced
bread. The butter was nearby and Tommy had
already buttered one slice for himself and one
for Molly. 'I like it. I have lots of friends.'

They had an agreement. Molly cooked and
Tommy would wash up afterwards. It worked
out well. Tommy loved his sister's cooking
and he clearly felt good about contributing by
cleaning up the dishes that he very carefully
washed and dried.

Molly smiled as she carried the plates to the
table and Tommy dropped his head closer to
smell the hot food on the plate she had placed
in front of him.

'Yum,' he said with a big grin. 'My favourite.'

'I know,' she replied as she sat down, put
her napkin on her lap and gave a little sigh of
relief to have survived a day that had begun
so terribly. 'I bought enough for two nights so
we can have it again on Wednesday.'

'Wow, we must be millionaires!'

Molly laughed. 'Not quite, but I did get a pay rise on my first day.'

All was good in the world, she thought as she looked over at her brother, who was enjoying the food she had prepared. He was eating the vegetables first as he always did so he could save the best for last. Conversation was at a standstill as Tommy was concentrating on the task in front of him. Sitting in the happy silence they shared, Molly knew that there was nothing she would change except to one day provide a larger home for them both.

At that moment, the six-forty-five train raced past so close the windows rattled and she amended her plan to ensuring their new larger home was in a quiet suburb and out of earshot of a train line.

The next morning as they both left on time for work, Molly noticed Tommy watching her intently as she locked the front door. It was still bitterly cold and they were both rugged up against the chilly morning air, but at least it wasn't raining.

'Is everything all right? Did we forget to pack something?' she asked with a bemused look.

'No,' he told her without hesitation.

'Is there something you want to tell me… or ask me?'

'I have a girlfriend.'

Molly spun on her heels to face him, completely blindsided but thrilled by his announcement. Suddenly it made sense. That was the reason Tommy had been paying more attention to his appearance and so excited to get to work. She wasn't sure what the title *girlfriend* exactly entailed or how serious it was, but her brother was obviously very happy so she wanted to tread carefully.

'That's wonderful.'

'Honey's pretty.'

'I bet she is and she has a very pretty name.'

'She's clever. We eat lunch together every day.'

'That's lovely.'

'She's not tall but I don't mind.'

Molly smiled as she slipped the house keys in her handbag, zipped it closed and together they walked to the gate. 'She doesn't need to be tall. I'm sure she's just perfect.'

'She is perfect.'

Their steps were a little slower and she playfully pulled his shoulder closer as she became acutely aware that her brother was a young man apparently falling in love. He was a loveable and wonderful young man and she prayed the young woman was just as sweet.

Suddenly she felt an unexpected ache in her chest as she realised perhaps it wouldn't just be Molly and Tommy in the future. It was bittersweet and she was so happy for Tommy. Perhaps her brother had found a sweetheart to share his life. It made the moments they shared even more precious. She had been through some heartbreaking times with Tommy and their bond had become even stronger. Because they had each other to lean on they had survived and she had not considered a future without him right by her side.

But now she had to think about it. With all her heart, Molly hoped that his feelings were reciprocated. She was thrilled that Tommy might have found someone to love and he deserved that. Everyone deserved to feel loved.

With the beeping of the bus horn by the waving driver, Molly was snapped from her wandering and somewhat jumbled thoughts. Maybe for Tommy it was just a simple infatuation, not a lifetime commitment, she reminded herself. She really was getting ahead of herself.

Molly readjusted his backpack. She couldn't stop herself from fussing over him the way she always had.

'I'd love to meet her one day.'

'I will bring her home for tea. Maybe lamb chops,' he said, not bothered at all by his big sister's fussing. 'She looks like a princess.'

'She sounds lovely.'

'I know her favourite flower and her favourite colour,' he told her before he leant in for Molly to kiss him goodbye. He didn't kiss her back but he did allow her to plant her lips on his ruddy cheek. 'Bye, Molly.'

'Have a lovely day, Tommy,' she called out as she watched him climb onto the bus and take his seat.

Molly tried to peer through the window to see if he was seated next to the lucky girl, but Tommy had taken a place on the other side so whether his girlfriend was on the bus or not she wasn't sure. But the moment he had stepped inside the bus she couldn't help but notice that he was smiling from ear-to-ear.

Walking briskly to her bus stop, she thought ruefully that perhaps one of the Murphys would be lucky in love after all.

And the other one had a well-paid job for at least a month.

CHAPTER FIVE

'OF COURSE I don't mind if you buy a new dress. You're my date at the AMA dinner to-night and I want you to have whatever you want. Buy two if you like and get some shoes and a bag too. I put my credit card on your bedside cabinet this morning. You were still asleep when I left.'

As she hung her heavy winter overcoat in the closet near the kitchen, Molly felt a tug at her heart hearing Ryan speaking so warmly on his phone to the woman he was apparently taking to dinner that night. It was Friday, her fifth day working in the practice, and, as much as she didn't want to admit even to herself, with each day her admiration for her boss had been growing; realising that Ryan had a woman in his life had an unexpected effect on her.

She had kept her distance in an effort to control the way she had reacted to him in the kitchen that day. She knew any stirring feelings she had would lead nowhere. While her body was reacting to him, she was resolute that she didn't want to ever get involved or make herself vulnerable again. She wouldn't survive another heartbreak so she wasn't interested in even thinking about a relationship.

Standing there in the hallway, she couldn't help but wonder, if all of that were true, then why did she feel a twinge of jealousy?

She had made small talk but kept it to a minimum and kept him at arm's length so she had more control of her emotions, but still hearing him speaking that way to another woman had affected her.

While she could try to label her feelings as an appreciation of him as a doctor, she knew she had stepped outside those boundaries. She couldn't deny it.

He worked long hours and after he finished consulting at the practice, and he had visited all his home rounds, she noticed on his calendar that he had two hours put aside from eight to ten o'clock three nights a week to provide medical services to a residential care facility for single mothers. For a young, eligible medical practitioner, his life could have been very different, but instead of leading a hectic social life, Ryan appeared to be dedicated to his profession and providing services to those who needed him most.

Molly realised it was more than simple admiration and she didn't want to feel that way, particularly as she overheard the conversation that morning. She hadn't wanted to eavesdrop but she couldn't hang her coat anywhere else and she had hoped to make a coffee before she started for the day. She heard him laugh and wondered about the woman's response.

The woman with whom he'd obviously shared the previous night as he'd dropped his credit card beside her bed while she'd still been sleeping.

Molly pulled the knitted woollen cap from her head and absent-mindedly ran her fingers through her hair, all the time wondering what his date would look like. Against her better judgement she let her thoughts wander. She mentally pictured the woman lying across satin sheets, in her silk lingerie. Perfectly waved, long blonde hair, no doubt. Beautifully manicured nails. She felt fairly confident she knew the type of woman who would be the perfect match for Ryan in looks and sex appeal.

The antithesis of herself, she thought with a sigh as she self-consciously flicked her slightly frizzy curls away from her face.

She no longer even window-shopped at

high-end boutiques. The variety of stores she frequented had nice neat clothes, they were simple, with hundreds of the same style hung in racks all over the city in every size, but they were new and clean. She had different priorities. Designer clothes and accessories weren't included.

'My tux is at the practice, so I'll change here and whizz by about seven to pick you up,' Molly heard him say. She did wonder if she wasn't moving more slowly than needed so she could hear just a little more about her boss and his date. She knew that, against her own will, Ryan was having an effect on her, and it was borderline masochistic to hear him talking to another woman but her curiosity was piqued. Where was the elegant soirée to be held? She knew that AMA was the Medical Association dinner so no doubt it would be at one of the city's five-star venues and the ladies would be dressed as if they were to meet royalty. Like a twenty-first-century Cinderella ball. But there was no fairy godmother for Molly and the only pumpkin she would see was in the soup she and Tommy would be having for dinner that night along with home-made shepherd's pie.

Maybe it was good to hear the banter, she reminded herself, as it also made her realise he was taken or a player, which either way set the boundaries for her. And with her feelings escalating for the man little by little each day, she needed the reality check. Ryan McFetridge was never going to be more than her boss.

'No. Of course, I don't want to rush you. Sure…uh-huh…okay, I'll pick you up at seven-fifteen so you have time to get back from the hairdresser and get dressed.'

Of course I don't want to rush you… You must go to the hairdresser, Molly repeated in her head as she rolled her eyes.

She cringed as she shut the closet and made her way to her desk, shaking her head. She didn't resent the woman, or want to be her, she reminded herself sternly. But as she shuffled down the corridor the sinking feeling that wasn't subsiding made her wonder if that was true.

Life for Molly was getting back on track but there was something about the way Ryan made her feel whenever he was close that she needed to manage. And hearing conversations like that should have made it easier. But for some reason it hadn't.

Her day would have to begin without caffeine as she didn't want to intrude further on the intimate conversation. There was no doubt in her mind that there might be some parts she didn't need or want to hear before she started work. Molly had lots to do that day and listening to any more discussion and giving any more thought to the woman's preparation for the evening she was going to share with Ryan was just too much to handle.

The first two hours went smoothly with most of the patients arriving and leaving on time. Molly had continued to make small changes to the appointment scheduling to make the process even more time efficient. She felt confident as she listened to the patients call in that she could schedule sufficient time for each consultation so that Ryan wouldn't be running late, but not so much that she would waste any of his day. She doubted Ryan would have noticed if he was running either late or early as his mind seemed to be elsewhere. More than likely on his date that night, she surmised.

'Tell me a bit about yourself, Molly. Apart from being an anaesthetic nurse who wanted a role with better hours, I know nothing.'

Molly almost jumped out of her skin. She hadn't seen Ryan standing by the window as she'd walked into the kitchen for a glass of water.

She softly coughed to clear her throat. 'There's not much to know, really.'

'I don't believe that.' His arms folded across his broad chest and his look was one of curiosity. 'There's not a hospital within this state, or this country, that wouldn't snap you up in an instant. May I ask if your desire to have regular hours is due to a child or ailing parent?'

'Neither.'

'I appreciate your right to privacy in your personal life, so if my questions are intrusive, we can just leave it there.'

Molly studied the man standing so close to her that she could quite literally reach out and touch him. He was handsome, intelligent and the love he had for his daughter was palpable. She wasn't sure if having a teenage daughter meant that Ryan was hiding his age well or he had been a very young father. But it didn't matter. It was none of her business. Dr Ryan McFetridge had a close, loving relationship with his daughter, was wonderful with his patients and…had a hot date for dinner that night, she reminded herself. But she didn't want to be rude and not answer the man who had freed her from Joel's lecherous plans.

'It's family,' she replied. 'The reason I need a position with regular nine-to-five hours is my brother, Tommy.'

'He's young, then?'

'No, Tommy's twenty-five, but, like Lizzy,

he has Down's syndrome and I'm his sole care-giver. He likes routine and he's happiest when I'm home before he is dropped off from work each night, so I need a job that allows me to give him that.'

Ryan didn't say anything for a moment but Molly watched as he nodded his head in a knowing way.

'I had no idea, but then again, why would I?'

Molly shrugged in response. Silently she agreed. Why would he? Molly's life outside the practice bore no interest to Ryan. He had a daughter, a full professional schedule and a girlfriend, so the frizzy-haired temp's life would hardly be of any concern to him.

'I understand completely. I'm all the family Lizzy has too so I pretty much work around her needs. I guess we have a lot in common.'

'I suppose we do,' Molly replied politely, all the while thinking they had very little in common.

'But I wouldn't change it for the world,' he added. 'She's a blessing and I'm so grateful to have her in my life.' He drew a deep breath and looked intently at Molly. 'No doubt you feel the same.'

'Yes, I do,' she told him as she looked down at her food to avoid his gaze. He was much too close and the room suddenly became much too warm. 'Knowing that I will be there every night when his bus pulls up makes him happy. He doesn't like changes or surprises. Lizzy no doubt doesn't like surprises either.'

'Hates them,' he said, rolling his eyes. 'She has to know everything, days ahead.'

Molly nodded. 'I found that if I can reassure Tommy that nothing will change, then his anxiety levels don't rise and he more than copes— in fact he exceeds all expectations put on him.'

'You clearly understand how to manage the challenges he faces on a daily basis.'

'Not all of them, but I do my best. Tommy is the most loving brother a girl could have and I feel lucky to have him.'

'I'd say he is very lucky to have you. He chose his sister well,' Ryan said, then paused, deep in thought. 'Well... I'd best get back to work.'

'Ditto, I have quite the pile of correspondence that I need to process.'

It was just before twelve when Ryan came and perched casually on the corner of her desk. There were no patients as he was running a little early.

'I have a huge favour to ask you,' he began.

Molly spun on her nicely padded leather chair. She was enjoying the quality of her seat, as it certainly was an improvement from the last temp assignment that had seen her perched on a rickety stool that had seen better days. She wished immediately that she had not turned to find him so close yet again. His face, freshly shaven, was almost irresistible. Her eyes traced the line of his chiselled jaw down to the cleft in his chin then up to the softness of his lips.

Damn, why could he not have been the wrong side of seventy instead of the right side of everything?

'And what would that be?' she enquired while dragging her gaze back to the computer screen. She couldn't allow herself to be drawn into his eyes.

'I'm going out to the AMA dinner tonight.'

'Yes, I know...' Molly blurted out, then blinked nervously at her admission to over-hearing a private conversation. 'I was hanging up my coat this morning and briefly heard something about it.'

He paused for a moment in silence. Molly noticed that the leg not supporting him began casually swinging.

'My *date* for tonight is struggling to find anything to wear and I was wondering if you might meet her in the city and help her to find something.'

Molly's face turned back to his and she

stared at him in gobsmacked silence for a moment. She couldn't mask her surprise and only barely her displeasure with the idea.

'Really? Me?'

'It's the Australian Medical Association annual dinner so I want something classic, timeless yet fun and age-appropriate.'

Age-appropriate? Was he dating a college student? A hideous suggestion suddenly became monumentally worse. Molly had to find a way to diplomatically decline the request to assist. It wasn't part of the job description so he could find someone else to do it. Perhaps the campus counsellor could accompany her, she decided with heavy dose of sarcasm colouring her thoughts.

'It's fairly obvious to say that I'm not a fashion plate. I think you could find someone much more suitable for the task.'

'But she asked for you.'

'Me? Why on earth would she ask for me? I don't know your girlfriend.'

Molly watched as Ryan's lips formed a smirk and he began shaking his head and almost chuckling. She did not like that he found it amusing, when she found it more and more disconcerting.

'For your information, Molly, my date tonight is not a *girlfriend*. I'm taking Lizzy to the AMA dinner. I thought she would have told you that when you were chatting about her shoes…and *yours*,' he said, referring to her first day's odd choice. 'Anyway, you made quite the impression on her that day and I feel, after our chat about Tommy, that Lizzy would be very safe in your hands. She's taken a real liking to you, which she never does that quickly. You know the challenges she may face and you can help her through them if they arise—perhaps she senses that. You definitely have a rapport.'

Molly was momentarily speechless, almost wanting to kick herself for thinking and saying what she had. She had not considered Lizzy could be his date. Her version of the story was based on nothing much but her own wild, and slightly jaded, imagination.

'You would make such a difference and I would really owe you if you'd agree,' he continued. 'I left my credit card beside her bed this morning while she was still sleeping but she had no one to go with her to the stores. She's worried she won't find anything and she's getting very upset. She took a cab to the local shopping mall about forty minutes ago and she's struggling. Her grandmother couldn't go with her today and Lizzy doesn't cope well with making decisions on her own and I don't want her to get overwhelmed and decide not to go tonight. It's happened before.'

Molly felt so silly. Once again, her assumptions about her boss were so far from accurate.

'I completely understand, Molly, if you don't feel comfortable with the idea. You have a lot on your plate and I don't want to add to it. Honestly it's not in your job description so I'll call the store and ask them to send a few things to our home and she can make a choice there.'

'No,' Molly cut in.

'It's fine, honestly, Molly. It was wrong of me to ask…'

'No, I didn't mean to hesitate. I'd love to help Lizzy to find something very pretty and age-appropriate for tonight.'

'You're sure?'

'Yes. I assume you've checked with the boss, and he's okay with me taking time off from here,' Molly added with a smile. Was she smiling because Ryan hadn't been speaking to a love interest earlier? She wasn't sure, but something was making her happy.

Ryan returned the smile. 'Perfectly happy and very grateful. I've already checked with Stacy and she's happy to stay on for the afternoon. She's finished her influenza immunisations for today and is not needed at the other practice so it's all set…with your approval.'

'It seems like you covered everything so I'll head off, then,' Molly said as she stood up.

'Not quite,' he said, reaching into his pocket. 'Take these.'

Molly watched as he handed her his car keys. The fact he would entrust her with his car was pleasantly surprising but her heart began to race when the warmth of his fingers touched her hand ever so briefly.

'I'll cab it home after I finish here and then Lizzy and I can drop you off at your place on the way to dinner.'

'There's no need, really,' she replied, very aware of her pulse quickening.

'I'm being a little presumptuous here—I'm hoping after you find Lizzy her outfit you might drive her to the hairdresser at three-thirty as she might get distracted and not make it there on time without company. She's pretty good generally but it's a lot to fit into one day.'

'Of course,' Molly told him. 'I'm happy to take Lizzy to have her hair done and then get her back to your place. Where exactly is your place?'

'Thirty-four Lincoln Avenue, Unley Park. I'll send it in a text to you.'

Molly sighed. Of course it was in Unley Park. One of the nicest suburbs in Adelaide, filled with palatial homes, manicured gardens and tennis courts.

'That sounds great. I'll need to get home by five o'clock, which is well before you'll be leaving for the dinner. That's when Tommy gets home.'

'Of course,' he said. 'I don't want you to be late home. I'm incredibly grateful that you're helping out and I don't want to cause any anxiety or problems for your brother.'

Molly noticed Ryan staring at her but she didn't feel judged. She actually felt appreciated and it had been a long time since she had felt that. She could see that, along with everything else, Ryan was a good and kind man by the consideration he was showing towards Tommy. Her fiancé had never been understanding of Tommy's needs, or hers for that matter. She acknowledged Ryan's response with a smile that was coming from her heart but once again worrying her head immensely.

Their eyes locked for the longest time in silence and Molly was not sure where the conversation would lead. Finally, Ryan broke the spell she felt herself falling under.

'I guess it's time you took off if you're to help Lizzy.'

'Yes, of course,' she answered as she reached

down to the drawer to collect her handbag. 'I will try to bring the car back in one piece...'

'I would hope so. I only picked it up from the dealership two weeks ago.'

'Then I will try extra hard,' she said, with her lips forming a soft smile as she headed to the closet and collected her coat.

Ryan followed close behind.

'Where is Lizzy exactly?' she asked as she opened the back door to the staff car park.

'She's at the Eastern Hills Mall and she'll be at one of these boutiques,' he said as he handed Molly a piece of paper and then headed back in the direction of his office. 'I wrote down the names and the phone numbers for you. They know Lizzy well and usually make it easy... apparently just not today, for some reason. But I'm sure, once you arrive, she will relax and find some lovely things. And, Molly, if you need to leave before I arrive home, please book a cab from my place to yours and charge my card. It's the least I can do for you,' Ryan called down the hallway to her.

'Sounds perfect.' Molly was relieved that Ryan and Lizzy wouldn't see where she lived. It was on the very wrong side of the tracks and she didn't want their pity as they dropped her off before heading to their black-tie dinner.

Looking down at the keys in her hand, Molly

smiled. She closed the door and made her way to the shiny new BMW in the car park feeling happy. Not with the car, although it was very nice; it was the trust and confidence that Ryan showed in her to help his daughter. They would have fun, she felt certain. And Lizzy would look gorgeous.

'Molly. I can't find a dress. Dad will be sad if I don't find a dress.' Lizzy was clearly distraught when Molly arrived. Ryan knew his daughter only too well.

'Hello, Lizzy,' Molly said as she drew closer to a very desolate young woman sitting by the change rooms of an exclusive boutique. 'That's why I'm here. I'll help you find a dress. And a very pretty one.'

Lizzy scratched her head nervously. 'There's no red dresses.'

Molly bent down and, dropping her voice, she said, 'There's other stores here—perhaps one of them will have a red dress. We don't have to buy a dress from here.'

Molly noticed Lizzy's frown soften and the hint of a smile forming. 'Will we find one?'

'I think we will,' she told her. 'And it will be the prettiest dress in Adelaide. Shall we get shoes to match?'

'Uh-huh,' Lizzy said as she climbed to her

feet. Molly thanked the sales assistants for their help, explained the need for a red dress and, together with Lizzy, left the small store.

It didn't take too long before they found another boutique with a wider selection of after-five wear. Floor-length gowns, some that skimmed the calf and a few sparkly mini-dresses were all in the store window. 'This looks perfect,' Molly said as she led Lizzy inside.

'May I help you?' the sales assistant asked as she approached.

'Yes, Lizzy's looking for a gown for a black-tie dinner tonight. And she would love one in red.'

'Mmm... I think I may have something for you. Are you about a size fourteen?'

'Yes,' Lizzy replied, coyly. 'I like sparkles too?'

'It's a little sparkly, but not too much,' the older woman replied with a warm smile. 'I'll go and fetch it from the back and you can let me know if it's sparkly enough. It was on hold for two days but that time was up at nine o'clock this morning. You're welcome to take a seat or look through the other gowns. I'll be right back.'

The woman disappeared, leaving Molly and

Lizzy in a sea of gowns decorated with sequins, lace and faux fur.

'You should buy a dress,' Lizzy said to Molly as she sat down on a high-backed gold velvet chair. 'But not red.'

'I'll look to fill in time, but I won't buy anything.'

Molly admired the stunning gowns. And she tried not to gasp when she saw the swing tags. Each one seemed to be more expensive than the last. Her eyes fell upon an emerald-green halter gown with the most delicate beading. She pulled it out and swung it around as if she were dancing with it. Lizzy laughed as Molly swayed and dipped in time to non-existent music.

'I have that in your size,' the second sales assistant said.

Feeling a little silly that she had been seen by someone other than Lizzy, Molly came back to her senses. 'Goodness, no,' she said, shaking her head as she hurriedly put the dress back on the rack and sat down beside Lizzy. Molly Murphy knew that she could not afford to buy a dress costing anything close to nine hundred dollars. She hadn't spent even a tenth of that on anything for herself in a very long time. 'I'm here to help Lizzy find a dress. I'm not looking for anything for myself.'

At that moment, the older woman returned carrying a pretty red dress with a scooped neckline, cap sleeves and red and silver beading on the shoulders. 'I knew we had something in red,' she announced, not hiding her pride in recalling the dress that matched Lizzy's description. 'Please come with me and I can help you to try it on.'

Lizzy jumped up with glee. Molly was so very happy to see the expression on her face. They made their way to the elegantly decorated change rooms and the woman hung the dress up and unzipped the back. Molly smiled at the sight of the reproduction antique chair with black satin upholstery adjacent to the floor-to-ceiling mirror. Next, she noticed a gold-framed Kandinsky print hanging near the clothing rail. She knew the piece, it was from 1920, and one of her favourite pieces by the artist. Her gaze then dropped to two pairs of black patent leather heels on a small shoe rack. It was the perfect change room indeed. The type the Molly of late saw in her dreams.

'And you try on the green one, Molly.'

'No, Lizzy. I'm not trying on a dress. Today is about you, not about me,' Molly replied as she backed out of the room and headed to the blue velvet sofa. She was going to put her feet up for a moment while Lizzy changed. She hoped the dress fit as Lizzy really did have her heart set on red and sparkly.

'Pleeeeeeease try on the pretty green one,' Lizzy pleaded. 'Then we will both be princesses. Please.'

Molly smiled. Lizzy's honesty was so sweet, just like Tommy's. No hidden agendas, no game-playing, just saying exactly how they felt.

'But you are pretty so you should have a new dress,' Lizzy told her. 'Then you can find a boyfriend.'

The older woman arched her eyebrow and looked at Molly with a smirk. 'I think you may not have much of a choice. Can you let me know which one…?'

'Here it is,' the second assistant said as she swept past them with the stunning gown draped over her arms and placed it in the adjacent change room. 'I saw you dancing with it earlier.'

Molly cringed at the thought of how ridiculous she would have appeared dancing with the gown but she was impressed with the woman's customer service. No doubt she had great sales figures, the way she moved so quickly to place the dress in Molly's possession. Pity the poor woman, Molly thought, because, despite her nimbleness, there would be no sale.

Molly had neither the intention nor the money to make the dress hers.

And on top of that Molly Murphy would have absolutely nowhere to wear a dress like that.

'Fine… I'll try it on…' Molly faltered. 'But after this we are going to find shoes and a bag for you, Lizzy.' Molly tried to make her voice a little stern and serious. Ryan had entrusted Molly with the task of finding his daughter a dress, shoes and bag and that was exactly what she would do after she tried on the gown waiting for her in the equally elegantly decorated change room.

Her chair was upholstered in beige satin and two pairs of nude patent leather heels were beside the mirrored wall. And the artwork, *Mountains and Sea* by Helen Frankenthaler, complemented the colour palette of the tiny space perfectly. Molly loved abstract art and apparently so did the store interior decorator. Everything about the store was perfect and for the first time in a long time Molly thought her life was heading that way too.

'We need to find you a dress—that's an order given to me by your father. We need to remember he's my boss, so I can't let him down.' She smiled as she closed the door, then took a deep breath as she looked at the softly draped fabric that would be against her skin for only a few minutes.

A few glorious minutes.

'My goodness.' The sales assistant gasped. 'That dress was made for you.'

Molly shook her head in response as she stepped out of the change room. She was un-accustomed to compliments. Lifting the hem of her dress so she didn't catch her heels, she made her way to Lizzy's door. One of the two pairs of the shoes were in her size so she had slipped them on and it made the hem skim the floor perfectly, but she was still a little nervous of catching the expensive fabric.

The dress felt wonderful against her body but she knew the feeling would be fleeting. 'Hardly made for me. I'm more your jeans and T-shirt type.'

'Well, you should seriously consider broad-ening your wardrobe choices,' replied the older assistant. 'You look simply divine and the gown fits you like a glove.'

Molly ignored their flattery. The dress mo-mentarily made her feel special but she could not afford to be swept away by it.

'Do you need some help with the zipper, Lizzy?' Molly asked as she knocked on the door to Lizzy's room.

'Uh-huh,' came the reply and the door opened enough for Molly to slip inside.

A moment later Lizzy stepped out in her red dress with the sparkles and did a little hesitant twirl, holding the sides out as if to curtsey, and the three women gasped with delight. The dress skimmed her ankles so it was still formal but wouldn't need any adjustment to the hem. Molly had worried that, with Lizzy being just over five feet tall, there might be some very hurried alterations to anything she chose.

'You look just like a princess,' Molly said in delight.

'Beautiful, just beautiful,' the other women cried in unison.

Then the younger assistant added, 'And I have a silver beaded bag that would be just perfect.'

'Do you like it?' Lizzy asked Molly, then continued without taking a breath. 'I like it a lot. My boyfriend will like it too.'

'I think you will be the prettiest girl in the prettiest dress tonight.' Molly walked back to her dressing room and quickly emerged with the credit card Ryan had given her. 'Please charge Lizzy's dress while I change so we have time to find shoes.'

'You look so pretty, Molly. Will you buy that dress?' Lizzy asked excitedly.

'Not today.' Molly smiled and thought with a price tag like that she wouldn't buy the dress that day nor any day in the future.

With Lizzy's dress carefully wrapped and slipped inside an oversized carry bag, along with the beaded clutch that Lizzy also liked, the two shoppers left the store and went in search of shoes, but not before Lizzy made a call to her father and told him all about the red dress. Molly stepped away so they could have a private conversation. She heard Lizzy giggling and it made her heart sing to know how happy the young woman was with her purchases. She watched her nod a few times and then hang up the phone and walk over to her with a skip in her step.

'So, your father's happy you found a dress?'

'Uh-huh,' Lizzy replied with a broad smile and then, holding on tight to her special purchase, she walked over to a store with some pretty shoes in the window.

Molly followed behind quickly and together they stepped inside the upmarket boutique with designer shoes and beautifully groomed sales assistants. Lizzy picked three styles and sat down while the store assistants disappeared in search of the shoes. Suddenly Molly noticed a worried expression replace Lizzy's happiness.

'I don't feel well. I want to go home,' she announced as she stood up and left the store. Molly quickly followed her to a seat in the shopping mall. Lizzy's face was flushed and she was very agitated. A change had swept over her with no warning.

'Of course,' Molly said, sensing the young woman was overwhelmed. 'I'm sure you have pretty shoes at home you could wear tonight anyway.'

'I'm not going.'

Molly sat down beside her and patted her hand affectionately. 'Maybe after a rest you'll feel better.'

'I can't go. I need medicine for my tummy,' Lizzy said and inched her hand away.

Molly tilted her head a little, confused by what Lizzy had said and her abrupt change in demeanour.

'I'll take you home, then, and you can get some rest.'

'I want Dad. Dad knows what I need when I get the pain.' Lizzy's voice was beginning to spike. Her anxiety was palpable.

Molly stood up and reached around for her phone within her handbag. 'Of course, he does,' she said softly as she dialled the surgery number and Stacy put her through to her new boss.

'Hi, Molly, did you find everything for Lizzy so she's all set to attend the dinner?'

'Yes, and no,' Molly began, then lowered her voice as she turned away.

'Yes and no?'

'Well, we do have the dress and Lizzy loves it but now she is quite distressed, needs some medication and says you will know what it is. I think I can guess what's happening but she doesn't want to talk to me about it. I assume she's having her period.'

Ryan sighed into the phone. 'She gets embarrassed and doesn't like to talk about it. I'll catch a cab to you. She won't be able to go anywhere. Where are you now?'

Molly looked around to quickly find a landmark Ryan might know. 'We're two stores down from the information kiosk. Not too far from the valet parking entrance.'

'Okay,' he began. 'Please stay put and I'll be there in less than ten minutes. Please stay by her side. I don't want another episode.'

Molly heard the line go dead.

'Is Dad coming?'

'Yes,' Molly told her in a calming voice. 'He's on his way. He won't be long at all.' Molly wasn't sure what Ryan meant by another episode. She assumed it was that time of the month for Lizzy, but she wouldn't ordinarily call that an episode. She sat by the young girl's side and chatted about things that would keep her distracted. A puppy passed them by dressed in a matching outfit to her owner and that made Lizzy smile for a few minutes until they disappeared into one of the upmarket boutiques and out of sight. Suddenly Lizzy's stress began to escalate again. Molly wondered what was causing the panic attack as at nineteen she surely would have experienced numerous periods. Perhaps it was that combined with the idea of attending the dinner, she mused. It was disappointing that Lizzy was feeling so unwell, as she had been quite excited to buy shoes to match her princess dress.

'You know, Lizzy, I had terrible periods too. The worst and then as I got older they improved.'

'They did?'

'Yes. It's still not a fun time but it's not so awful any more.'

Lizzy seemed a little happier with the news Molly had given her but she was still terribly distressed.

'There you are.' A familiar husky voice coloured by concern came from behind them. Ryan knelt down in front of Lizzy and affectionately stroked her forehead.

'I want to go home,' Lizzy said loudly as she looked at her father with eyes so sad they melted Molly's heart.

'That's why I'm here. I'll take you both home. Let's get you both to my car.'

Molly knew she shouldn't be embarrassed by her home but she still had some pride so she was horribly embarrassed and she couldn't change the way she felt. 'Truly, it's okay, you take Lizzy and I'll get a cab.'

Ryan looked at Molly and she felt a shiver run up and down her spine. She was being drawn towards him once again and it was unnerving. He had rushed to his daughter's side like a knight in shining armour and that only compounded feelings that were already growing for the man on one knee.

'It's the least I can do.'

'No, seriously, you take Lizzy home, get her settled and get yourself ready for the dinner.'

Ryan shook his head. 'I'm not going to the dinner. My date's unwell.'

'But you're getting an award,' Lizzy replied.

'An award?' Molly asked Ryan with a curious frown.

'Well, an award of sorts.'

'Of sorts?' Molly replied, taken aback by his casual response. 'The AMA don't give awards of sorts at their annual dinner. It must be something special.'

He reached for the shopping bags. 'I'm being presented with the AMA State Award but I can call through my apology tonight and send a thank you email tomorrow. They can courier it over next week.'

Molly knew how prestigious it was to be nominated, let alone win an award that was voted by medical peers. 'Then you have to be there,' she said. 'I can stay with Lizzy and keep her company and you can go and collect your award.'

'I'm not going to fly solo. Besides, you have to be home for your brother.' Ryan kept his eyes on Lizzy. 'I assume you parked the car underground.'

'Yes, in the bay nearest the escalators.'

The three of them walked in the direction of the exit to the car park. Ryan's arm was around Lizzy.

'Tommy would be fine watching television for two or three hours,' Molly added. 'I just like to make sure he's had a good dinner, but then I could head over to your place in time for you to leave and keep Lizzy company.'

'Sooty can stay. You can get your award,' Lizzy announced.

'Sooty?' Molly said with an enquiring tone,

having no clue who Sooty was or what Sooty might be. Perhaps it was the family dog. There was clearly so much that Molly didn't know about Lizzy and Ryan, and that wasn't surprising after such a short time, yet she also felt an unexpected level of ease being with them. A realisation swept over Molly that it felt almost natural to her for the three of them to be together outside Ryan's practice. It was a strange feeling but she couldn't deny she liked it.

'Sooty is Lizzy's grandmother. Her real name is Ann.'

Molly couldn't help but wonder how Sooty was an abbreviation of Ann. It didn't come close.

As if he read her mind, Ryan continued as they walked together. 'Lizzy adored the British television show *Sooty*. She and Ann would watch it together regularly. One day Lizzy told Ann that she wanted to call her Sooty instead of Grandma. It just stuck. All these years later she calls her Sooty and she even signs messages to Lizzy with that name.'

'That's wonderful. Is she your mother?'

'No, she is Lizzy's maternal grandmother,' Ryan told her as they stepped off the escalator and headed towards the car, which was just outside the sliding glass doors. 'She's a lovely lady, we get on well now, but there were some issues early on. Fortunately, we moved past the challenges we faced.'

Molly assumed it had something to do with Ryan and Lizzy's mother parting ways but she wasn't going to ask questions that weren't her business.

'Ann's house is about fifteen minutes away from ours so she stays over if Lizzy needs her and I have to work back and the three nights that I visit St Clara's.'

Molly reached into her bag and handed the keys to Ryan without him asking. She knew that St Clara's was the residential care for single mothers where Ryan consulted three nights a week.

His fingers brushed hers as he took the keys from her upturned palm. Once again, his touch made her heart skip a beat.

'Please let me drive you home,' he implored as the remote unlocked the car doors. 'Lizzy will be fine once I get her settled in the car and give her some analgesics. She just panics if I'm not around when this happens.'

'No, honestly, I want to pick up some fresh bread to have with dinner anyway. I'll get a cab from over there.' She pointed towards the cab rank and began slowly walking in that direction, then paused to check that Ryan and Lizzy were okay. She wanted to ensure they got away. Molly's maternal instincts were kicking in where Lizzy was concerned. She felt a bond had formed from the moment they met. She couldn't explain why and it defied logic but it was there nonetheless.

'I want Sooty,' Lizzy announced as Ryan held the car door open for her and she climbed in. The pain was clearly growing and, with it, an increasing level of distress.

Molly watched as Ryan secured his daughter's seat belt and then, standing upright again, he paused. Molly couldn't hear the conversation but he kept raising his eyes and glancing over in her direction and nodding. Then she watched as he made a very brief phone call. Molly shifted a little, feeling slightly uncomfortable. She didn't know what was happening and whether she should go or stay.

Molly noticed Ryan's expression suddenly change from concern to something she didn't quite understand as he shut the car door, then slipped his mobile phone in the inside pocket of his overcoat and crossed to her without saying a word. He looked almost nervous, his eyes randomly roaming the car park. It was an expression she hadn't thought a man like Ryan would ever wear.

'Molly,' he began, then paused as his fingers

ran thoughtfully across the cleft in his chin. 'I have a second favour to ask of you today.'

'Sure, anything,' Molly replied without hesitation, in a way that completely surprised her. She had not imagined she would ever think let alone say those words to a man after everything that had happened to her.

Ryan looked relieved by her reply. 'Is there the possibility…that perhaps *you* might accompany me to the awards dinner at the convention centre tonight? I know it's short notice but I'm hoping you might consider it.'

Molly had to steady herself. She had no idea what to say. But by the intense look on his handsome face only inches from hers, he was clearly not going anywhere until she gave him her answer.

CHAPTER SIX

MOLLY COULDN'T THINK what to say as she stood in stunned silence. Her mind was again spinning and Ryan McFetridge was again the cause.

'I must apologise,' Ryan said ruefully, bringing the silence to an end. 'It was presumptuous of me to think you would be free, it's just that Lizzy suggested it to me in the car and I had to agree it was a great idea.'

'I'm not sure… I mean, it's just not something I was expecting you to ask…' Molly hesitated and then decided, like Lizzy, she needed to be upfront. No game playing or hiding her situation. 'To be honest I'm not sure I can. It's just that I don't think I have anything suitable to wear on such short notice for a black-tie event.' Molly didn't think, she knew very well that she didn't have anything in her wardrobe close to what she would need for a black-tie dinner. With the pay rise she could go to a department store and find something but only if she had a few days to search the sale racks. 'I don't want to let you down but perhaps there is someone else you could ask.'

'Perhaps…but I would very much like to take you,' he told her. 'Please be honest, is the dress the only reason you can't make it? Would Tommy be okay alone?'

Molly knew the answer to both questions. 'Tommy would be fine, as I mentioned to you before, as long as I go home and prepare his dinner. He spends most nights watching his television programmes in his room but, that aside, I just don't have time to find something suitable. It's the AMA dinner, not dinner at a local café, so I would need to head into the city to find something and it's already almost three.' She paused. 'That reminds me—you will need to cancel Lizzy's hair appointment.'

Ryan tilted his head a little to one side. 'Do you always make sure others aren't put out?'

'Well, the salon might have a waiting list for clients and I don't want you to be charged for an appointment that Lizzy won't make.'

'I'm not sure how you manage to keep everyone's schedule stored front and centre, Ms Murphy.'

'It's in my job description.'

'I have to disagree on that. I'm beginning to

think that you go over and above.' He smiled. 'But if the dress is truly the only issue, then I have already solved that and I can pick you up at seven.'

'What do you mean you've solved that?'

'Well, Lizzy told me about a green dress that, according to her, made you look like a *princess.* I wanted to give you something in appreciation for you helping me out this afternoon and taking care of Lizzy, so I bought it for you.'

'What are you talking about?' Molly gasped. 'You bought me a dress? But I was very happy to spend time with Lizzy. You don't have to give me anything.'

'I wanted to give you something.'

'Fine, that's a lovely gesture, but chocolates or a longer lunch break one day this week would have more than been enough. A dress is definitely too much.'

'No, it's not, and apparently it looks lovely on you, according to my daughter. I must say she has impeccable taste like her father. It was going to be delivered to you at the office tomorrow but it's now on its way down here,' he said, looking behind him towards the escalators. 'Actually, perfect timing. I think this might be it coming down now.'

Molly turned around to see the sales assistant making her way down the escalators towards them.

'But, Molly, honestly, I do understand if you can't make dinner tonight. Let me know how you feel when you get home and if Tommy wants you to stay in or you're too tired after today's running around. Just call or text me… but I want you to have the dress anyway,' he told her as he stepped away towards the car. 'I better get back to Lizzy and take her home before the cramps set in. And thank you again. It would have been a disaster if this had happened when she was on her own.'

'Ryan, I'm not sure…'

'It's fine, Molly. If you can't make tonight, I'll see you at work tomorrow.'

Molly watched as Ryan quickly climbed into the car and then drove away, leaving her mouth gaping slightly.

'Hello again, Molly,' the sales assistant greeted her and handed Molly a black fabric garment bag and a white gift bag, both emblazoned with the store insignia. 'I put a pair of nude pumps in there as well in your size and a small matching clutch as Dr McFetridge said he wanted you to have everything you would need. He's such a lovely man.'

Molly was speechless as the smartly dressed sales assistant smiled and walked away in her very high black patent stilettos, leaving Molly with her own thoughts. So much had transpired in a few short hours. Molly wasn't sure how she felt about Ryan McFetridge except confused.

Very confused.

Staring straight ahead, a garment bag across one arm and the other holding the gift bag along with her handbag, she followed the signs to the cab rank. Her gaze was just a few steps ahead of her as she climbed the half a dozen cement steps to the street and the line of cabs waiting. Feeling overwhelmed and undecided as to whether she should even consider accepting Ryan's gift, let alone the invitation to attend the dinner, she kept glancing at the bags. Her steps were as considered as her thoughts as she put one foot in front of the other and made her way into the bitterly cold breeze.

She approached the first cab in line and the driver hurriedly jumped out, and, looking up at the heavy grey clouds and the imminent downpour, quickly took her bags and opened the door for her. Molly climbed in, still in a dazed state, and he shut the door and made his way to the other side and placed the bags on the seat beside her.

'Where to?' he enquired as he jumped inside the cab himself, secured his seat belt and pulled out into the traffic.

Molly gave him her address and collapsed back into the seat. Her mind was still spinning and she didn't much like where her thoughts were heading. She just hoped that Lizzy would be okay.

Three hours later, Molly dialled Ryan's mobile. It was almost six in the evening. It was dark outside as it always was in winter at that time, and Molly had the heater warming the living room and another on in Tommy's room. As she pulled back the drapes Molly could see the stars were sparkling in the midnight-blue sky.

Her first question was about Lizzy.

'Lizzy's fine, thank you for asking,' Ryan answered. 'She's tucked up in bed, and I've given her strong pain relief and she's resting her back on a hot-water bottle, with another one on her stomach. She finds the warmth comforting and it helps her to relax. And I called Ann over as she does seem to be able to make Lizzy feel less stressed about the whole situation. I guess it's a woman thing and Ann's the only mother figure Lizzy has in her life.'

Molly learned so much about Ryan and Lizzy in that one statement. Lizzy had no mother or other female relatives in her life.

And if there was a girlfriend, she wasn't filling the role.

'It's wonderful to hear that Ann is so close to Lizzy but I had no idea that Lizzy suffered from such chronic painful periods.'

'It's been like that from day one, but I must admit she is becoming increasingly anxious each month.'

'She's very lucky to have such an understanding father who just happens to be a doctor to help.'

'I'm not so sure she's the lucky one, but let's not go there,' he replied, then changed the subject. 'So, you made it home and out of the terrible weather? Battened down for the evening with a roast in the oven?'

Molly hesitated for a moment before she drew breath. 'Actually,' she began, 'I have prepared Tommy's dinner. Not quite a roast—it's soup and shepherd's pie.'

'Sounds delicious. I hope you enjoy it.'

'I'm not eating it…'

'Not hungry?'

'Yes, a little, but I thought, if you would like, I could accompany you to the AMA dinner.'

Molly waited for a response but there was nothing. Ryan's end of the line was silent. She suddenly felt very foolish. Perhaps he had already invited someone else. Her stomach dropped and she wished with her every being that she had not just told him she would like to be his dinner date. She thought she could hear the faint sound of his breathing but no words. She strained her ears but there was nothing. She had never felt that uncomfortable.

'Of course, if you'd rather not go or you already have another date, I understand—'

'No, Molly,' his deep, suddenly serious voice cut in. 'I would very much like you to attend with me. I just don't want you to feel pressured because you work for me or because of the dress. It was a gift and accepting my invitation isn't part of the working conditions. I want you to know that.'

Molly was taken aback by the change. His mood had morphed into something professional and considered. While she thought it was also very gallant of him to let her know there were no strings attached, he seemed to be putting distance between them. Making sure she knew where he stood.

'I was not accepting because you bought the dress…well, actually that's not true. I mean, I have an amazing dress hanging in my closet and nowhere else to wear it and you bought it, so technically I suppose I'm accepting because you bought the dress, but mainly because I think you should attend to accept the award. Lizzy would want you to attend so we can make her happy together. I mean, you can make her happy by attending and I can attend with you.'

Molly felt as if she was speaking at a hundred words a minute. And she was. It was her way to cover the nervousness and vulnerability she was feeling.

'Then, you're my date,' Ryan answered, then quickly amended his words. 'I mean, my guest.'

Molly was relieved that Ryan hadn't left her hanging again as she had initially felt borderline silly for calling and accepting his invitation, but she also picked up on his rapid correction from date to guest. 'I'm happy to be your *guest* and step in for Lizzy so you can accept your award. I'm sure she will be thrilled to see it when you get home.'

'No doubt. She's quite the organiser of my life at times.'

'Women can be like that,' she answered, and then continued. 'Speaking of that, I think it might be more time efficient for me to meet you at the convention centre. By the time you get through the traffic to me and then we get back to the venue, the canapés might be cold.'

Molly wished she weren't so self-conscious and embarrassed about her accommodation but she was and she didn't want Ryan's pity. The time was a factor but her suggestion was also to save face.

'I don't feel right about you finding your own way there. At least let me book a car to collect you.'

'Truly, it's not necessary. I will call a cab when I'm ready and meet you there.'

Molly convinced Ryan to meet her at the entrance to the convention centre at seven, then she hung up and quickly proceeded to get ready. She had forty-five minutes to shower, do her hair and apply light make-up. Molly Murphy was determined not to turn up looking like a drowned mouse in a nine-hundred-dollar dress.

Ryan checked in on Lizzy. She was tucked up in bed, having soup that her grandmother had prepared. Ryan had given Lizzy analgesics and Ann was sitting in a large reclining armchair beside her as the two of them watched television. It was the way it had been for many years. Ryan had bought the very comfortable chair as either he or Ann would sit there and read to Lizzy when she was younger and then as she grew older they would sit and talk about their days. Her room was large and yet still cosy.

'How are you feeling, Lizzy?'

'My tummy still hurts but not so bad as before.'

'Good, I'm sure Sooty's soup will help too.'

'Mmm, it's chicken noodle.'

Ryan looked at his daughter, who was half-distracted by the television and the soup. The pain relief had taken effect but it worried him that each month seemed to be getting progressively worse. He knew that he needed to talk through the options with Lizzy after their consultation with her GP and the gynaecologist. They both needed to seriously consider the options. While a hysterectomy was radical and something he had been wanting to delay or avoid altogether, he wasn't so sure now they could put it off for ever if the pain continued to be so debilitating for her. Together they had to make a decision that neither would regret.

While she hadn't mentioned getting married or wanting a baby in the future and her chronic pain was not going to improve, it still wasn't easy as a father to make the irreversible decision to take away that option for her. At times like that, he wished that Lizzy had a mother in whom she could confide and he had someone to help him make an important and life-changing decision with his daughter. He could not get it wrong. While his medical expertise was leaning towards ensuring her physical health came first, his fatherly concerns were around the future should she change her mind and decide she wanted children. Just when he got it straight in his head, sorted, decided…he questioned himself and decided being a single father to a nineteen-year-old girl was not that easy.

'Molly's agreed to accompany me to the dinner tonight if Sooty can stay and you're all right with me going out.'

Ryan watched as Ann nodded. 'I'm happy to stay and happy to see you finally get out and enjoy yourself,' she told him.

'Good, you get your award. I want to see it,' Lizzy said, then took another spoonful of the hearty soup. 'And Molly can wear the princess dress. She looks pretty.'

'And Molly is?' Ann enquired with a knowing smile and a sparkle in her eyes.

'My temp office manager.'

'And a pretty office manager by the sound of it. Princesses are always pretty.'

Ryan couldn't help but agree silently. Molly was a very pretty office manager.

'Then it looks like I'm going to dinner,' he told the two women, choosing not to confirm or deny Ann's statement or his own thoughts. Directing his attention back to Ann, he added,

'I'll leave the ibuprofen in the kitchen. Lizzy needs them four-hourly so another dose at eight o'clock and then hopefully she will sleep through the night. If you need me, don't hesitate to call my phone and I can be here in fifteen minutes.'

'Go and enjoy yourself,' Ann said, waving her hand. 'You don't get out enough. Go have some fun with your lovely date. It's about time you enjoyed company with someone closer to your own age. Lizzy and I'll have some quiet time and with any luck she'll be feeling better by morning and if not I'll stay with her tomorrow.'

'She's my guest, not my date.'

Ann raised her eyebrow. 'Let's not be pedantic, Ryan. A date or guest, it's the same in my books.'

Ryan chose to ignore her comment. 'Remember, call if you need anything.' His face was lined momentarily with concern. 'I mean it, please call if you need me and I will come home immediately.'

'Go, scat,' the older woman said with a grin. 'You're distracting us. We don't know who she's about to choose for her date.'

'What do you mean, choose for her date? Who's going on a date?'

'The bachelorette,' Lizzy said, pointing at

the television with her half-eaten bread roll. 'She's pretty.'

'Okay, you're talking about a television programme,' Ryan muttered to himself and nodded with relief. He had thought for a moment that Lizzy was planning a date and that Ann was in on it. And his daughter dating was the last thing he wanted to think about. Lizzy meeting someone and potentially falling in love was something he did not want to deal with for a long time. A very long time.

'Molly, you look absolutely stunning. Lizzy was right, that certainly is a *princess* dress.'

'Thank you,' Molly replied as she alighted the cab. Ryan had not met her at the entrance to the venue, instead he had been waiting at the cab rank for her. The night air was bitterly cold but Molly was not about to cover the beautiful gown with a black woollen overcoat, so she had a silk wrap that had once belonged to her mother around her shoulders. It was one of the few things she had kept for a special occasion and that night suited the bill. It wasn't the most practical accessory on a cold winter's evening but that night Molly had decided to throw being practical to the wind quite literally. Her curly dark hair was held back on one side by an antique silver hair clip, also a gift from her mother, and she had small pearl earrings. They were costume as she had sold her real jewellery but they looked very pretty and nothing too elaborate was needed. The dress was a statement on its own.

'Let's get you inside, quickly. You look gorgeous but I don't want you to catch pneumonia.' He extended his hand and Molly didn't hesitate to take it. It was a firm, warm hold as his fingers securely enveloped hers and it felt like nothing Molly had ever felt before. She swallowed nervously as her heart picked up speed. They didn't need to rush inside, she thought, as his touch was warming every part of her body. And she suddenly felt safer and warmer than she'd thought possible.

She lifted the hem of her gown with her hand that also held her clutch bag and the pair walked together to the entrance with all the other guests who had arrived like them right on the stroke of seven. Molly suddenly and unexpectedly felt at ease and as if she belonged there. Ryan had slipped his hand free of hers once she had both feet on the pavement but had offered his arm as her support and Molly had accepted. Her hand had rested there until they reached the doors. It all felt so surreal to Molly yet so surprisingly natural.

Once inside Molly pulled her silk wrap from

her shoulders. It was a Cinderella moment as she walked among the guests with her very handsome and wonderfully considerate dinner companion. The expensive dress was making her feel so special and with little effort Ryan was doing the same.

'Would you like some champagne, wine or sparkling water?' the black-and-white-attired waiter enquired of both Molly and Ryan.

Ryan waited for Molly's response, which was champagne. She watched as he took a flute filled with bubbles from the tray for her and a red wine for himself.

He introduced her to a number of people as they made their way through the crowd. He didn't say how they knew each other or that she was his employee. She was simply his guest. The noise was building as the crowd grew. The doors to the banquet hall were still closed and the guests were all chatting and greeting each other. Molly could hear many talking shop and others speaking of their last vacation, their children or their impending retirement. It was a diverse audience but each somehow connected to the field of medicine, some on the periphery and some right in the middle of it. There were pharmaceutical executives and heart surgeons, Theatre nurses and podiatrists, paediatricians and medical students.

Ryan and Molly made their way to one of the large seating plans displayed on mobile boards. Ryan ran his eyes down the list until he found his name. Ryan McFetridge and Lizzy Jones were seated on table one. Molly saw it at the same time. It was the VIP table. Ryan's award really was something quite special, she realised immediately. And she was so happy he would be there to accept the honour.

'I just wanted to thank you again for accompanying me tonight, Molly,' Ryan stepped closer to tell her before they moved away for other guests to find their names and table numbers on the lists. There were twelve hundred in attendance that night and thankfully more than half had already been seated by the roaming stewards with mobile seating apps.

'My pleasure. And I wanted to thank you for…' She began looking down at her gorgeous gown. She still felt a little uneasy that he had bought the gown and she wished she had been in a position to buy it for herself but she wasn't about to allow regrets of the past colour that evening. She had a gorgeous gown and an equally gorgeous date for the night. And she would deal with the rest tomorrow. The way she always did.

'Please, you have nothing to thank me for at all. It was my pleasure and I can see by quite a few of my colleagues in the crowd tonight it is their pleasure to see you in that gown.' He had an impish smile that Molly had not expected to see but it was a pleasant surprise. 'By the way, I have to admit I'm one of them. From a man's point of view, it's rare to find intelligence, humility and kindness in a woman, and for that matter the population in general, let alone all three qualities along with looking so gorgeous.'

At that moment, the doors opened and the crowd slowly moved en masse in the direction of the banquet hall. It became quite congested, and without warning Molly felt a warm hand in the middle of her bare back, gently guiding her into a clearer pathway.

'Over here,' she heard him whisper in her ear. His breath was warm on her neck and she felt a little shiver run all over her body as she followed her escort for the night down a different route to their table. His flattering comment seemed genuine and, she trusted, without an agenda, and it made her feel special. And it had been a very long time since a man had truly made her feel special.

'You've navigated this room before, I assume?' she asked with a smile as they avoided the crowd and headed to the front of the room. Her heart was beating so fast and she hoped her face wasn't flushed by the effect he was having on her. Silently she admitted she didn't want the feeling of his hand on her skin to end. She would have gladly walked around the room twice just to have the feeling continue.

Alarms should have been ringing but they weren't.

Part of her still wanted to fight her feelings but a bigger part wanted to give into them.

'Maybe once or twice,' he replied with a wink.

Molly's heart picked up more speed as he looked at her so intently she felt as if he were almost touching her soul. The skin around his dark eyes wrinkled softly and a sparkle emanated from somewhere deep inside. Suddenly she was the furthest thing from the damp mouse. Molly Murphy felt like a desirable woman on a date with a chivalrous man. An extremely handsome, chivalrous man who was taking control of the situation, and her feelings were at odds with everything she had thought for the previous twelve months.

And she liked the feeling very much.

And she liked *him*.

CHAPTER SEVEN

THEIR BEAUTIFULLY DECORATED table was positioned directly in front of the large stage and lectern. The stunning centrepiece of sharply angled frosted glass panels surrounding a tall vase of white lilies was lit by a dozen small tea lights. Molly had noticed one arrangement on each table but as she drew closer she appreciated the detail and effect, and thought it was the most spectacular centrepiece she had ever seen.

Ryan pulled out her chair for her to sit before seating himself, and immediately began introductions. Molly quickly found out he knew everyone at the table.

'I'm so glad you could make it, Ryan,' said one of their fellow table guests, who Ryan had introduced as Martha Zontos. Molly imagined the beautifully groomed woman to be in her early seventies. Her powder-blue satin dress was the perfect soft contrast for her short silver-grey hair and the delicate crystal necklace and earrings completed the look.

'The board of St Clara's are so grateful for what you have given to the young women and I know acknowledging you is very important to them.'

Ryan nodded. 'It's a good cause, Martha, and I'm in a position to support them.'

Molly watched as the woman cast her eyes around the room. 'Many in this room could provide support, Ryan, but they don't, and that sets you apart. You are one in a million.' She patted his hand and then turned back to continue her conversation with her husband.

Molly eyed her boss curiously. She realised that there was even more to appreciate about Dr Ryan McFetridge. Including the fact that he was philanthropic as well as gallant.

'So,' she began as she reached for the glass of water in front of her. 'You're a sponsor of St Clara's.'

'Of sorts.'

'It's a great initiative.'

'Couldn't agree more. Young women need to have a place after they give birth for a few days, a week or even longer, and a place they can call in at any time for advice. There are so many pressures facing a single mother, like family opinions, immediate financial issues, not to mention the fear of the future and the unknown. St Clara's helps them to navigate through what they will face with assistance from professionals instead of their peers, who generally know very little and sometimes add to the overwhelming fear some young women face or make light of very real struggles that someone their age without a child can't fathom. The objective is to prevent them from finding themselves at that point where they feel that they have nowhere to turn and have to consider giving up their babies.'

Molly couldn't help but notice Ryan's demeanour become more serious and a little distant after he spoke. His attachment to the words was palpable. She could sense immediately that there was something very personal in what he was saying.

'I wish it'd been in existence twenty years ago but it wasn't, and perhaps it wouldn't have changed every baby's fate, nor should it as there are wonderful couples who want to adopt.' He shifted in his seat as he spoke and then reached for the glass of wine that the waiter had filled moments before. 'And there's no point wanting to change the past. It's quite pointless.'

'Cheers to that,' Molly answered, watching

him throw back his drink and raising her water glass in response. She didn't want Ryan to know just how much she agreed with his sentiment although from a very different perspective. She had not faced being a single mother. But as the carer of her brother, she was a *single sister*, she thought, and at times she had struggled and still did and on so many occasions she thought she could and should have done so much better.

And on her choice of a fiancé, she definitely wished she could change the past but knew it was pointless to waste time dwelling on that disaster. But it still seemed to find its way into her every waking moment.

'The food is always lovely here,' a voice whispered as Molly had turned in the woman's direction, snapping Molly out of her melancholy and back to the wonderful evening that lay ahead. She was there to support Ryan and make Lizzy happy that her father would collect his *award*. An award that Molly now assumed had something to do with a generous donation to St Clara's.

Molly was seated at a table filled with VIPs of the medical profession and she quickly reminded herself just how honoured she felt to be there.

And equally honoured to be Ryan's *guest*, although by the minute he was making her feel far more like his *date*. And past mistakes deserved no headspace tonight. She intended to enjoy herself and forget everything else for just a few hours.

The evening was perfect, the food and wine delicious and Molly could not possibly finish each course. There was a neonatologist key-note speaker from the Netherlands, and as the applause finished Ryan leant in towards Molly. 'With your background that must have been quite informative. The surgical intervention, I mean.'

'Yes, Dr Swinton is brilliant and the new methods are revolutionary. It will change the outcome for many neonatals.'

'Do you miss it? Theatre, I mean.'

'I guess, hearing about progressive proce-dures does make me excited and a little sad not to be a part of it, but—' she turned to meet Ryan's gaze '—I wouldn't risk Tommy's peace of mind for my career. Not now or ever.'

'You're an amazingly selfless and beautiful woman, Molly Murphy.'

'I don't think so…'

Without warning, she felt Ryan's mouth drawing closer to hers, cutting short her words as her own lips instinctively reached up to accept his kiss. Then she stopped. She froze and moved away.

'I'm sorry,' Ryan said, moving away. 'I overstepped the line. Please forgive me, Molly.'

Molly couldn't speak for a moment. She wanted to kiss him but she couldn't. Something was holding her back. And that something was her past.

'There's nothing to forgive, Ryan. It's difficult to explain…but please believe me, it's not you.'

Molly could see that Ryan wasn't convinced.

'Would you like to dance?' she asked as the band began to play.

'Perhaps later,' he said, putting distance between them as he pushed his chair back from the table and she could see him preparing to stand. 'I might just step outside and make a call. I'd like to check up on Lizzy if you don't mind. I won't be long.'

Molly nodded. 'Absolutely.'

Molly wasn't sure what to think as she watched his broad suited shoulders disappear into the crowd. She wanted so badly to give into the feelings Ryan was stirring but she wasn't sure if she was ready. She felt as if they were moving so fast and, while it was wonderful and unexpected, it was like standing on a precipice and suddenly looking down when all the while she wanted to look up to what might be.

'I would like to present the Australian Medical Association lifetime achievement award to Dr Ryan McFetridge, the founder of St Clara's Respite Hub for Single Mothers.'

Molly's mouth dropped open a little. Ryan was not purely a supporter of St Clara's. He had single-handedly founded the initiative. As she watched him stand and button his tuxedo, then make his way to the stage, she suddenly felt her eyes lift upwards a little more. Perhaps she was right to feel the way she did. Perhaps it was time to let go of the fear. At least a little.

'Congratulations, Ryan. I had no idea,' Molly said when Ryan returned to the table, his stunning blue-crystal award in hand. It was etched in gold and standing on a base of black marble and clearly heavy as he placed it on the table with a slight thud.

'Thank you,' he returned with a half-smile, but still Molly could feel there was a distance between them. A distance she had put there by rejecting his kiss. His banter was light-hearted but he was no longer leaning into her. His body language was telling her where she now stood.

And she couldn't blame him. She had set the boundaries by moving away from his lips.

She had never felt so torn. There were moments when the man she had only known for five days made her feel as if she had known him all her life. Or perhaps she had been looking for him all her life. He was an amazing human being but she was scared. He was so humble in downplaying his involvement in a cause and yet the medical association thought it deserved a lifetime award.

She was so proud as she watched Ryan's peers give him the congratulations he deserved. They all knew him or of him. He was the man of the moment in the room, being swept up by the throngs of people wanting to connect, and she felt overwhelmed just watching him manage the conversations. Now and then he took time out between handshakes to look in her direction. To check in with her. But when she caught his glance he looked away. As if he didn't want to be watching out for her and didn't want her to know he had been.

'Nurse Murphy…' a voice broke into her thoughts. 'Well, you certainly look very different without a Theatre cap. Perhaps they should change the dress code in Theatre—that gown is so much nicer. Not at all practical, but so much nicer.'

Molly turned to see Dr Victor Rodriguez. He was one of the state's leading vascular surgeons and Molly had been in the operating theatre with him on more than a dozen occasions.

'Dr Rodriguez,' she replied, not masking her genuine elation at seeing him again. It had been over a year since she had been at the Eastern Memorial Hospital.

'Please, you make me feel so old—call me Victor.'

'Of course.' She smiled as she stood and extended her hand to greet him.

Victor stood and, ignoring her hand, gave a hearty laugh and a gentle bear hug.

'How long has it been since I've seen you?' he asked. 'Actually, I know exactly how long. It would be close to a year since you left the Eastern Memorial. That's when Gertrude came on staff as your replacement. Good God, that woman can talk, and has an opinion on everything that she insists on sharing.'

'Are you talking about Gertrude Rodriguez? Your daughter?'

'Yes, one and the same, and, yes, she's my daughter but she takes after her mother. Drives me mad with that incessant chatter.'

'I studied with Gertrude, Victor. She's so lovely and a great anaesthetic nurse.'

'I'd never debate her skills. It's the nonstop talking. She could talk underwater, a bit like that ex-fiancé of yours, what was his name, Norman? No, that's right, Nigel. I always struggled with his name on the few occasions that I met him. Anyway, he was quite the talker, and a bit pretentious.'

Molly suddenly felt violently ill. Her stomach dropped and her heart felt heavy. The lightness of the evening was quickly disappearing.

'I guess…' she replied, feeling disturbed with the direction of the conversation. As much as she had been happy to see Victor Rodriguez, she did not want to talk about the past right now. It had been a wonderful night and she wanted to stay in the moment and not be drawn back into sadness or regret.

'So how is everyone at the hospital?' she asked, hoping to steer the conversation away from her personal life. She wasn't sure where she wanted it to land but it wasn't on her failed relationship.

'Everyone's great, a few newbies on the roster.' He paused as he ran his fingers through his silver beard, then continued, 'You know, we'd love to have you back there. You're one of the finest anaesthetic nurses, hands down, and we miss that level of expertise—'

'I'm sure you have other anaesthetic nurses,

including Gertrude,' Molly cut in, trying to end the conversation without appearing rude.

'They're all very competent, including Gerty, but still not close to your skill. I mean it, Molly, just mention you're interested and you'd be back on staff within a heartbeat.'

'I have family priorities, Victor, so, as much as I appreciate your offer, I won't be thinking about returning for quite a while.' Her tone was kind but firm. She really did not want to travel back in time that night or have her decision to change the direction of her career questioned. That chapter was closed. For now, at least. She wanted to get back on track without causing any further disruptions to Tommy's life. It had been difficult for Tommy when Nigel had left their lives so abruptly and, while Molly knew he was a bad man, in fact the worst, she felt immensely sorry for Tommy as he too felt the sadness of losing someone.

'Is your family commitment your brother? Is he all right?'

'Yes, on both counts,' she answered quickly, disappointed that Victor was delving into her personal life and not leaving well enough alone. She had never remembered him to be so intrusive but it hadn't bothered her before the break-up. Previously she hadn't had too much to have embarrassingly unpacked by others the way Victor was doing at that moment. Her life had not been without the usual sadness along the way but there had been no scandal prior to Nigel.

Hoping she could bring the conversation to an end she added, 'Tommy likes me to be home every night at a set time, so as I said it will be a while before I can return to the hours of an anaesthetic nurse in a busy teaching hospital.'

'I understand but take or leave this fatherly advice. I heard you lost the house when Nigel left your life and the Eastern Memorial is yours for the asking…and the remuneration of the position would get you back on your feet quite quickly. I don't want to see you struggle, Molly. It's no secret you lost your home because of him.'

At the exact moment that Victor's inappropriate and unexpected words poured from his mouth, Ryan returned.

Molly felt her heart sink and her body stiffen. She couldn't believe that Victor would speak so openly about her personal life in a public forum. She suspected she looked like a deer in headlights with the shock of his announcement to all and sundry. Up to that point the evening had been a fairy tale but it had just ended. The whole ugly episode in her life that she had somehow managed to forget for a few wonderful hours came rushing back… and it had happened at the moment Ryan had come back.

She had hoped the wonderful evening might have continued but suddenly the clock had just struck twelve.

CHAPTER EIGHT

'CONGRATULATIONS, RYAN. IT's been a while. Well deserved on the award.'

Molly couldn't believe her luck or lack thereof. Not only had Victor, with his fatherly intentions, emptied her dirty laundry onto the floor of the elegant event for everyone within earshot, including Ryan, to hear, he also knew Ryan. She suddenly wanted to run from the room. But she didn't want to lose a slipper along the way. She didn't want Ryan to feel obligated to hunt her down. She didn't want or need his pity. Her Cinderella moment was well and truly over. She just wanted to be alone as quickly as possible. She edged away from the two men, her finger absent-mindedly tracing a line on the table, listening intently to the conversation but not really wanting to hear very much. She hoped against all hope her name would be left out of any further discussion between them.

'Thank you, Victor. It has been quite a while since we've caught up. How are you?'

'Good, very good, just trying to convince this young lady to return to the Eastern. We miss her and her skill set terribly.'

Molly froze as two pairs of eyes looked in her direction. She shrugged in response and attempted to smile politely, but it was more like a slight curling of her lips that quickly fell flat again. She felt at risk of breaking down and wasn't sure how long she might be able to delay the welling tears. It didn't seem to matter how much she tried to move past everything that had happened, it seemed to be only two steps behind.

'Best damned anaesthetic nurse I've worked with hands down.'

Ryan shot Molly a knowing look. 'I told you, Molly, there would be offers to take you away from…my practice.'

'So, you know each other?' Victor enquired curiously, obviously unaware they had been seated next to each other the entire evening.

'Yes, Molly's temping in admin at my practice.'

'Well, young lady,' Victor continued, as all the while Molly hoped more than ever that the surgeon and his pearls of wisdom would just leave, 'it would appear that you're in demand.

I'm not surprised but, at the risk of sounding disrespectful to you, Ryan, Molly runs the risk of being wasted and losing her skills if she doesn't use them.'

'I will take that under advisement, Victor,' Ryan replied. 'However, there's somewhere Molly needs to be so I'll have to steal her away.'

Molly sensed that Ryan had seen how anxious she had become. She was unsure if he'd heard anything but appreciated him coming to her rescue.

'I'm hoping you don't mind me taking you away from Dr Rodriguez, aka the best-meaning but most times inappropriate advice provider of the Eastern Memorial,' Ryan said as they walked away.

'Not at all. I'm relieved, to be honest, but where do I need to be exactly?'

'I'd say anywhere but with Victor.'

Molly's lips curved into a smile that remained without any hint of fading. 'Would you like to go somewhere else for a quiet drink?'

His voice was deep and husky and his eyes intense and focussed just on her.

'That sounds wonderful.'

Suddenly the memories that Victor had stirred began to fade. She was aware the evening would end in a few hours but she didn't want to dwell on that. She felt more special than she had in a very long time and she felt protected. And it was the best feeling in the world.

Taking off his jacket, Ryan draped it over Molly's shoulders and they left the event without any goodbyes or further ceremony and made their way down North Terrace to the large hotel that had a quiet coffee lounge and bar.

The concierge greeted them both with a nod. 'Are you guests staying with us or are you just looking for a quiet late-night drink?'

Molly was taken aback by the question and she could see that Ryan was equally confused by the remark.

'Just a drink...or coffee... I'm not sure we've decided yet,' he answered, looking at Molly for confirmation.

'I'm fine with either.'

'It's just that there's a visiting rugby team celebrating in the hotel tonight and if you're looking for a quiet place, I'll be honest, it might not be in the bar,' the concierge told them with a concerned expression.

'Thanks for the heads up,' Ryan said with a grin as he directed Molly inside. 'We might settle for a coffee, then, in the lobby.'

Ryan stepped into the warm lobby and

quickly settled Molly into a chair near the large water feature that reached up into the four-floor-high atrium. Molly craned her neck to see the flow of water gently running over the copper backdrop from such a height. It was strikingly beautiful.

Scooping up his tuxedo jacket that Molly had placed over the arm of her chair, he placed it on the back of his own chair and was just about to seat himself when another elegantly dressed man approached them. He had a clean-shaven head and a neatly trimmed beard and Molly hadn't noticed the man at the event but suspected, with his tuxedo and polished appearance, that there was a good chance he too had been at the AMA dinner.

'Ryan, good to see you.'

'Brian, great to see you too,' Ryan responded, then, standing again, he turned his attention back to Molly. 'I'd like to introduce Molly Murphy. Molly, this is Brian Chesterman. Brian's a GP practising not too far from me in Erindale. To be honest, I'm not sure how long we've known each other but it's been a damn long time.'

'Pleased to meet you, Molly,' the man responded and extended his hand to Molly.

'Pleased to meet you too,' she replied, meeting his hand politely.

'So, Ryan, how's Lizzy?'

'She's good. In fact Molly took her shopping today to buy a dress to wear this evening, but then she wasn't feeling well so Molly graciously accepted my invitation to attend in her place.'

'That was very kind of you, Molly,' Brain remarked with a smile in Molly's direction before returning his attention to Ryan. With a frown dressing his brow, he continued. 'Nothing serious with Lizzy, I hope.'

'No, just the usual problem she suffers every month, but she'll pick up in a day or so and be back to her happy self. We're seriously considering our options as each month she experiences heightened anxiety and chronic pain. It's a difficult choice. I don't want to rush into it but nor do I want to see her suffer every month the way she does.'

'Of course, the myriad changes that girls face as they become young women…and the choices we all need to make. On that topic, any boyfriends on the horizon? I remember how I dreaded the thought as both of our girls were growing up. They're both married now, the youngest only three weeks ago, but the very word boyfriend strikes fear into the core of every father at some stage.'

'No boyfriends, thank goodness. I'm hoping that I won't have to deal with that issue. Lizzy's happy with her life the way it is and I don't see that changing. She has work and her dog and I'm home most nights with her, so she has a pretty full life and that's why I'm contemplating referring her for the surgery. It would, without doubt, improve her quality of life. She hasn't given any indication of having an interest in boys, let alone marriage in the future.'

'Ah, the ramblings of a man who doesn't want to face the prospect of his little girl falling in love.'

'Lizzy's case is a little different, so I may not have to worry about that.'

'Don't be so sure,' Brian remarked. 'Everyone needs love. Lizzy's no different. And you, my friend, might just have to accept that fact one day.'

'We'll see,' Ryan said, studying the floor for a moment as he shifted on his feet.

'Yes, you will.'

'By the way, I didn't see you at the AMA dinner but I'm assuming you were there?' Ryan continued, brushing aside the comments about Lizzy and prospective suitors.

Molly could see Ryan was becoming a little anxious about the topic and could tell he wanted to change the subject and shrug off

Brian's comments. She knew it would be a difficult decision for a father to make. A hysterectomy was major surgery and there was nothing reversible about it. Ryan would have the weight of the decision on his shoulders. There was no easy way around it nor no right or wrong decision. But she knew in her heart, Ryan would do what was best for his daughter.

Molly suddenly felt awkward knowing that Lizzy did in fact have a boyfriend already. She had confessed as much to Molly the day they first met at the practice. She hadn't taken it seriously but she now wondered if Ryan would, as this wasn't going to be a future scenario Ryan would need to face, it was already on his doorstep; he just didn't know it. And could Lizzy having a partner potentially alter her mind about the surgery?

It was becoming a little complicated. Molly had had no idea when she'd made the promise to keep Lizzy's secret that Ryan was her father. She'd assumed Ryan would soften on the subject once Lizzy told him but now she wasn't so sure. She just hoped Lizzy told him sooner rather than later. Christmas was still quite a way off.

'Yes, Jane and I were there. We were on the table with the board of the university.'

'Interesting company.'

'Of sorts. It can get a bit dry at times and Jane is great at making conversation with everyone. That's the joy in having a wife in the same field. While it can be challenging with two careers in one household, the mutual passion for medicine is what's kept us so close all these years. Speaking of which, it's our twenty-eighth wedding anniversary tonight so I booked a suite here for the night, but unfortunately we won't be staying.'

'Congratulations on your anniversary but why are you leaving? I hope there's nothing wrong,' Ryan asked with concern clear in his voice.

'No, nothing wrong per se, it's just that our son-in-law called about fifteen minutes ago to say our eldest daughter's in labour in the Fleurieu Community Hospital so Jane and I are heading there now. Jane's with the concierge having the car sent around and I'm about to check us out. There goes an exorbitant amount of money for a room we were in for all of thirty minutes. But our first grandson is on his way and that's more important. The obstetrician estimates the birth is a few hours away but you never can tell with these things, *as we know*, and Jane wants to be there and I'm not about to argue with a grandmother-to-be. She's already booked us a hotel room in Victor over the Internet so we're off. It's just over an hour's drive from here but at this time of night there's no traffic so we'll be there before eleven. Anyway, I'll catch you at the next dinner, Ryan, if not on the golf course. And it was lovely to meet you, Molly.' Brian extended his hand to Molly as he spoke.

'Very nice to meet you, Brian,' Molly added.

At that moment a number of the rugby players spilled from the bar into the lobby restaurant and with their appearance came the noise. They were all large men, clearly chosen for their athletic build, and had been drinking. While they were not offensive in their language, their antics and voices were overpowering.

'Ryan,' Brian began, pausing mid-step as he played with the key card to the room. 'I just had a thought. I've already paid for the suite and we just ordered a late supper and charged it to our room and they can't cancel it. Why don't you and Molly head up and enjoy the martinis and tapas or order some coffee? There's no point letting the room go to waste and I don't think this crowd is leaving any time soon. It could get worse, by the look of the tray of drinks heading this way. You could escape up there for a while and can check out after you've had supper or stay the night. As I said, it's all covered anyway and there's a fantastic view of the Torrens river and the Adelaide Oval bridge from the room. In fact I'm quite sure I paid a significant amount extra for said view! It's quite spectacular and completely going to waste tonight.'

Ryan did not respond, although Molly suspected by the expression on his face that he appeared to be considering the offer. Or perhaps the ramifications of the offer.

'Here's the key card to the room,' Brian said, leaning down and dropping the card on the low gunmetal and glass coffee table. 'Clearly your call, and if you don't want to use the room I'll call in the morning and check out online but the offer's there. It's all paid up, so you can take it or leave it, but I better run as I'm getting the death stare from Jane standing outside in the freezing cold. And it's going to be colder at Victor so we're going to call into home on the way and collect some warmer and slightly more practical clothes. The poor child might take one look at me and mistake me for a penguin in this outfit.'

Ryan laughed and shook Brian's hand before the excited grandfather-to-be crossed the atrium and exited the hotel to where his wife was standing beside the late model European sedan. Ryan and Molly watched him climb inside and drive away. Before either could make mention of the room, one of the rugby players close by suddenly collapsed. He had been sitting on the arm of a large armchair and, without warning or obvious cause, he toppled over, hitting his head as he crashed to the marble-tiled floor.

Ryan and Molly jumped up in unison, crossing to the lifeless figure sprawled across the floor. Blood was seeping from a deep wound on the top of his shaven head. Mindful of not moving the victim, and without saying a word to each other, Molly checked his airway was clear while Ryan attended the wound. It was a deep gash and Ryan suspected his skull had been fractured when the weight of his head hit the hard marble flooring.

'He wasn't fooling around,' one of the other players called out. His words were slurred but the panic in his voice was evident. 'He just collapsed. I swear no one touched him. He just fell sideways. He's not dead, is he?'

Ryan and Molly both shook their heads as they continued their assessment of the man who was breathing but unconscious. A concerned concierge swiftly crossed to them. 'What's happened here?'

'We need an ambulance. We have an unconscious male, pupils are dilated and non-reactive,' Ryan announced as he lifted the young man's eyelids. 'I don't think it's alcohol alone that caused this accident. There's something else at play here. I need clean white sheeting immediately and a first-aid kit until the paramedics arrive.'

The concierge called triple zero immediately and then called Housekeeping without questioning Ryan or Molly further.

Molly had her fingers resting gently on the carotid artery in the man's neck to check his pulse while she observed his other vital signs. 'Respiratory patterns don't appear altered and he has reasonable skin colour. What I wouldn't do for a non-rebreather bag to keep his pulse ox reading at ninety-five per cent.'

A uniformed hotel staff member appeared almost immediately with the sheeting and the first-aid kit, which the concierge opened and placed beside Ryan.

Ryan quickly sterilised his hands and then passed the solution to Molly before he reached in for some sterile bandages. He ripped the packaging open and wrapped a bandage loosely around the open wound. The lack of hair made it easier to keep the wound clean.

A crowd of the patient's drunken friends began to gather around. 'I need the most sober of you to step forward,' Ryan said loudly and firmly. 'And the rest of you get back and give us room to help your friend.'

A tall, well-built man moved towards Ryan. 'I'm Jack. I'm diabetic and don't drink.'

'Did you see what happened?'

'Yes, Dave fell sideways like they said. He wasn't drunk or messing around. I think he only had one beer because he had a headache. He'd been complaining of it all day.'

'Did he receive a blow to the head during a game today?'

'No, he didn't play today but he did take a hit two nights ago at training and, yeah, he did last Saturday too. He was complaining today about it so the coach kept him on the bench.'

'So, this man suffered two blows to the head a few days apart?'

'Yes.'

'How old is he?'

'He just turned eighteen last week.'

'Perfect age for it.'

'Are you thinking second impact syndrome?' Molly asked as she kept a watch on his pulse and breathing.

'Yes.'

'Will he make it?' came a deep voice from behind them.

'I damned well hope so,' Ryan said as he began CPR.

At that moment, two paramedics came rushing through the atrium with a barouche. They collapsed it down to almost floor level and dropped to their knees beside the patient. Ryan moved away for them.

'Can you bring us to speed?'

'Dr Ryan McFetridge, GP, and Molly Murphy, anaesthetic nurse. We've been monitoring the young man for about five minutes now. Eighteen years of age, he's suffered two blows to the head sustained during sport a few days apart, a recent headache and a collapse without cause. I suspect second impact syndrome and potentially a subdural hematoma. His skull may have been fractured during the fall here tonight and it may have relieved some pressure as there was blood from the head wound. He has dilated and non-reactive pupils so I would advise you to hyperventilate.'

'Hyperventilate with suspected brain injury?' the paramedic asked.

'Yes, the benefit of temporarily reducing cerebral blood with mild hyperventilation may outweigh the harm from less oxygen delivery. My advice is to titrate the respiratory rate to maintain a reading between thirty and thirty-five or twenty breaths per minute until you reach Emergency.'

'The young man is lucky you were both here.

If he makes it, then he'll owe his life to that fact,' the older of the two paramedics told Ryan and Molly, then turned to the younger paramedic. 'Call it in once we're on board. ETA the Eastern Memorial four minutes.' Placing a brace around the young man's neck, the paramedics moved swiftly to transport the patient to the ambulance. Molly and Ryan watched as they exited the hotel entrance.

'Will Dave make it, Doc?' Jack asked.

'I can't say. The fact that he didn't collapse directly after the second blow is a better sign but he probably never recovered from the first injury so the second blow is a more serious complication.'

'But why? They weren't even related. The first one happened a week ago.'

'When an athlete like your friend suffers a second concussion before the first concussion has fully healed there are serious consequences. The fact that he cracked his skull may have in fact saved his life as the pressure building in his skull was released slightly.'

There was no siren as the ambulance drove off and Molly felt herself being pulled into Ryan's strong embrace. This time she didn't pull away.

CHAPTER NINE

MOLLY WASN'T SURE what Ryan was thinking. And she was even less sure what she was thinking about what had transpired.

The players made their way one by one over to thank them for helping their friend. While Ryan and Molly appreciated the show of gratitude, they were both drained by the experience and there were more of the players coming from every direction towards them.

'What do you think about slipping away and having a quiet drink and exhaling in Brian's suite?' he whispered to her. 'I think we deserve it and I don't think we'll get any peace here. They mean well, but it's been a long night.'

Molly nodded, feeling the adrenalin still surging through her body but wanting to escape from the commotion around them. 'That would be lovely.'

* * *

Ryan swiped the key card, opened the door to the suite they had been so generously gifted and stepped back for Molly to walk inside. The room was softly lit, and the curtains open, allowing them both to see the stunning panorama of the city lights. As she crossed to the expanse of windows, Molly looked out and down to see the reflection of the lights twinkling in the meandering city river below. It was picture perfect but she wasn't really seeing the view, she was thinking about what had transpired moments before in the foyer. She couldn't deny to herself that saving the young man's life had brought more purpose to her own. It was what she had trained to do and what she loved.

'You miss it, don't you?' Ryan asked her as he closed the door.

'What do you mean?' she said, turning away from the view and towards Ryan, but not wanting to admit to him he was right.

'The rush. The way you have to fire on all cylinders, think on your feet. The way it would be in surgery for you.'

'I guess. Yes. Theatre was my life but that career choice is not possible now. It doesn't mean it won't be one day, just not now.'

'Why not?' he asked as he dropped the card

on the coffee table and made his way to the sofa. 'Would you like to sit for a while? Maybe tell me what's changed so much in your life that you have to put your career on hold? I know you want to be there for Tommy, but I'm assuming you were there for him before. What's different now?'

'It's a long story, Ryan,' she told him, trying not to make eye contact and give too much away of how she really felt. 'Let's just say, I had more support before and none now.'

'I certainly can't sleep after what we just went through, so I'd be happy to hear more if you're willing to share it. I'm not going to hide the fact—I think you're an amazing woman, Molly, and I want to know more about you.'

Molly was taken aback by Ryan's honesty about his feelings. He was certainly a straight-shooter and it made her feel safe to open up. At least a little. She sat down on the sofa with him. There was enough distance that she could curl her feet up and spend the next fifteen minutes recapping her life, including her high school years, her study to become an anaesthetic nurse, even the pain of losing of her parents in a tsunami in Indonesia. She wasn't sure how much she intended on telling him, and decided to let it unfold and stop if and when she became uncomfortable.

'I'm so sorry, Molly. That must have been devastating for you and for Tommy.'

'And it was so unfair, it was my parents' trip of a lifetime. They had been planning to travel abroad and finally they felt okay about leaving Tommy with me. He encouraged them to go and gave them a list of souvenirs he wanted. Key rings from each of the places they visited. I took three weeks' leave from my role so that I could be at home for him to make sure he was all right and make sure they could relax and actually enjoy themselves and it all ended so horribly. Tommy's come to terms with it but it's taken a while. They were so young. Mum was only fifty-eight and my father was sixty-five. He had just retired two weeks before they headed off together. Life just hasn't been the same without them. It all went downhill not long after they died.' Tears began to pool in Molly's eyes and she quickly turned her head in the other direction, looking out of the window into the darkness. Suddenly she felt Ryan reach for her hand and encircle it in the warmth of his own.

'Life can be unfair. You can search for reasons and oftentimes none of it makes sense.'

Molly sighed. Ryan was right about that, but she also had to take responsibility for her choices in life as well. 'Sometimes we make stupid decisions too. We can't always blame the universe.'

'You sound like you're speaking from experience,' Ryan replied steadily, but not letting her hand slip from his.

Molly didn't want the process to be like pulling teeth for the man who had stated he valued honesty above all else. She hadn't thought she would share her stupidity with anyone else, ever, let alone Ryan. He was so sensible, his life so planned and thought out. And hers had been changed for ever by one stupid, avoidable mistake. But she couldn't change it by hiding it from Ryan. And it would be best to have it out in the open. If he thought poorly of her, then better at that moment rather than later when she had even more feelings invested.

'I became involved with someone, who wasn't good for me, or for Tommy. He was a bad man, plain and simple. I won't try to make excuses, or blame it entirely on him. I'm a grown woman and I should have known better but I think I was a little lost and, instead of getting stronger over the years after my parents passed, I think I became lonelier. I missed them terribly and that made me vulnerable and I didn't see the warning signs. In me or in him.'

Ryan's look intensified and Molly could see

anger simmering behind his charcoal eyes. 'He didn't hurt you or Tommy? Physically, I mean.'

'No, not at all,' she said, putting his fears of violence to rest immediately. 'No, he was a conman. A professional, completely unscrupulous conman who had worked me from day one but I was too silly to see it. I was too caught up in the fairy tale he was spinning to notice that it was all a cleverly planned charade to empty my bank account and more.'

'I'm sorry you went through that. I hope he was caught.'

'By me, yes, only after it was all too late, but he didn't pay any price with anyone else. He disappeared into the night and left Tommy and I without a roof over our heads. And that's why I'm angry with myself because I put Tommy at risk becoming involved with a man like that.'

'You didn't put him at risk intentionally.'

'Not intentionally, but that doesn't change the fact I behaved irresponsibly and we lost the house and the money that our parents had left us. It would have been enough to ensure Tommy never went without. I can't forgive myself for that. And that's why we live in a not so great part of town.' Molly rolled her eyes.

'I'm sure Tommy wouldn't care where you live as long as he's with you,' Ryan replied.

'That's true,' she said, shooting him a sideways smile that disappeared as quickly as it had arrived. 'But it still doesn't make any of it okay.'

'I don't mean to pry and you can tell me to butt out, but can't you pursue the man, your... ex, through the courts?'

In an instant, a myriad emotions washed over Molly. Rage, guilt, thoughts of how sweet revenge might feel and then sorrow. She knew it was hopeless.

'No, he walked away scot-free after taking everything he could and I had no means of retribution. I wanted to pursue him and make him pay for what he had done, but he left me in such debt that I didn't then and still don't now have the funds or the time to try to find him, let alone take him to court. He's over in Europe now. His father is Swiss, his mother Portuguese so he's hiding out in one of those countries or one somewhere in between, no doubt scamming another vulnerable woman.'

'Well, at least he might not be allowed back in Australia if you alert the authorities.'

'It's complicated because he made it look like I was complicit in everything.' She closed her eyes, wondering if she wanted or needed to go into the detail. Would it make him understand her true financial situation or make him doubt her previous judgement? She didn't want pity but it didn't seem to be on offer, which made her happy.

'After my parents died,' she began, turning back to face Ryan, 'Tommy and I were living in our family home in Burnside. It had been left to us along with insurance money, their savings and superannuation. All in all, we were very comfortable. Tommy worked at a not-for-profit organisation that provides employment for people with a range of intellectual disabilities. He still does. He could enter the regular workforce but he loves the support staff and they know what he's been through losing our parents, so they allow him to stay there and constantly build on his skill set, giving him more responsibility. He's in a supervisory role now.'

Ryan nodded in agreement. 'I'm sure Lizzy could take on a more challenging role too but she loves where she works three days a week, so I don't want to stress her unnecessarily.'

'I agree. There's no need. Those facilities go a long way to raising their confidence and independence and Tommy didn't need to bring in an income as I could support us both, but it was good for him to have that interaction. I was working at the Eastern Memorial. If I had a late shift, one of the elderly neighbours who adored Tommy would wait with him until

I got home and, if I was caught up in Theatre, she would prepare his dinner and stay and keep him company. She was a wonderful woman and we both felt blessed to have her in our lives.

'Then about three years after we lost our parents, I met a man while having dinner alone after a medical conference here in Adelaide. He was also eating alone that night at an adjacent table. He struck up a conversation and he asked to join me for coffee. He was new in town, an engineering consultant contracted to deliver advice on a billion-dollar infrastructure project. We hit it off, he seemed genuine and, although I was hesitant at first, we began dating.

'To be honest he was my first serious relationship, as it was difficult to even think about dating between my study and then taking on the carer's role for Tommy and work. I was naive and inexperienced but still at times I knew the decisions he made weren't right, and I should have listened to my gut. But I didn't. Six months into the relationship he proposed and we began planning the wedding. He said that he wanted to buy property together. He didn't want to live in our family home as he wanted a fresh start in a new home that we owned together. I wasn't sure about it but

Tommy had grown to like Nigel, and when he saw the house that Nigel had found had a pool and a home theatre he was excited about us having such a big house and living together as a family.

'After much deliberation and hesitation on my part, I agreed and I sold our family home and we bought the new home in the Adelaide foothills. It was quite expensive, but he said using the funds from the sale of my home and the money I had put away we could afford it, and then after he sold his home in Madrid he would deposit the funds in my bank and we would have put equal shares into what would be our for-ever home.'

'It sounds like a reasonable plan and, with the added pressure from Tommy, I can see why you agreed.'

'Well, Nigel had made it impossible for me to say no without appearing as if I didn't trust him. But after I sold my home Nigel insisted he had his name on the title as he said it would cost a fortune to add it after settlement when his money arrived. Again, my gut instinct was to say no, particularly as I thought the new house was overpriced, but he kept allaying my fears. He showed me his home online with a sale price of one point five million dollars and said it would only be a few weeks before it would be snapped up. Of course, that never happened because it wasn't his home. He had apparently found it online and claimed it to be his as it was in his hometown.'

'So effectively he gained a house in his name with no intention of providing any funds to you.'

'Yes, sounds stupid of me, doesn't it?'

'To someone who didn't know your fiancé and having no idea just how experienced a salesman he was, that's easy to say in hindsight. He manipulated your feelings to his advantage. It sounds like he rushed you off your feet and then cornered you. You really had no chance with someone like that. It was a chess game he was going to win.'

Molly stopped still for a moment. Suddenly and unexpectedly, the weight she had carried for the last year had eased from her shoulders a little. Instead of adding to her feelings of guilt, Ryan had somehow almost validated why she had made the decision that had impacted so badly on her life, and Tommy's. With a few words, he had made her feel less culpable and more a victim of another's actions. He was a stranger looking in and he saw it very differently from her viewpoint laden with remorse.

'But I'm still not sure how he took everything.'

'He forged my signature and borrowed against the house—'

'Why?' Ryan cut in. 'What did he do with the money?'

'He gambled it. All of it. And he left. He was gone. He left a note saying that he missed Madrid and his family and felt I was rushing him into marriage. It was one week before our wedding. I thought that he may have had a change of heart when I was woken the day after he left by loud knocking on the door. I thought he'd come back and misplaced his keys and wanted me to let him in. But instead it was a sheriff's officer. I was behind in payments on a mortgage that I didn't know I had. I knew all my money had been sunk into the house but I thought I could sell it, downsize to a similar home we had previously and we would be fine, but we actually had nothing. I collapsed in shock. There was no way I could possibly make the payments on my wage. I was forced to sell before the bank foreclosed. Within six months he had gambled more than half the value of the home. The market had crashed...'

'So, the already overpriced home he had made you buy was worth much less.'

'A lot less and with legal fees and paying for the wedding venue, flowers and car as it was too close to cancel there was literally nothing left in my bank. He'd assured me he had taken care of the wedding costs too and I had no reason not to believe him. But he hadn't. He'd only paid the deposit, so I had to fire sale the furniture and even my car and the jewellery my mother left me for the bond on this house because my credit rating had been ruined in the process. Oh, and cherry on top…when I tried to sell my engagement ring as I thought it would help, I found out that was as fake as his promises. A great copy of Harry Winston he bought online from China.' She sipped on her drink, took a deep breath and continued. 'I can't ask our former neighbour to travel to the wrong side of town at night. I made my bed and I must lie in it and make sure I am home every night in time to meet Tommy. And I wouldn't have it any other way.'

Molly was surprised that she managed to get it all out without tears. Tears of regret and anger at her ex-fiancé and herself. But she knew why. It was Ryan's reaction that made it possible to bare her soul and not react the way she had expected. She felt stronger with every word and that was because of him.

Without saying a word, Ryan leant into Molly and brushed away a tendril of her hair. 'The world has thrown the worst at you and yet you're still the most caring person I think I've met. At the risk of overstepping the mark, again, I wish I could kiss away all the pain you've been through. You're the most amazing woman, Molly.'

Molly felt her heart begin to race and she didn't want to turn away. She didn't want to hold back. She felt as if she belonged in the room, in the moment with him. And she felt safe. Leaning into him, she knew that whatever the night brought, she was welcoming it with her eyes wide open.

And her heart a little vulnerable. 'You wouldn't be overstepping the mark.'

Within moments Ryan's mouth reached for hers. His kiss was passionate and still tender. She felt his hands caressing the bare skin of her shoulders. Her eyes closed as the sensation of his fingers on her body rippled through her. Her mind was filled only with desire for Ryan.

Her eyes opened to find him looking expectantly into the soul she was laying bare.

'Are you sure about this?' he asked.

'I couldn't be more sure.'

Upon hearing her answer, Ryan didn't hold back. His lips were demanding as they met the softness of her mouth. Molly felt the urgency in his kiss and it took her breath away. It was nothing like the kiss before. His kiss told her that he was not a man who intended to wait for even a moment longer. Nor did Molly want him to.

His hard, powerful body lifted her up and pressed against her. She had no doubt in her mind that he wanted her as much as she desired him. His touch was strong yet gentle. His kiss was tender yet reckless. Her mind was spinning and her heart was racing with anticipation as his fingers searched for the zip of her dress and then the clasp at the nape of her neck. With both skilfully undone, he slowly slid the slinky dress from her body. Pulling his lips from hers momentarily, he began to discard his own clothes.

Molly's fingers struggled to untie his bow tie, and quickly his own hands came to the rescue, helping hers, and once it was undone, he tossed it to the ground. Molly unbuttoned his shirt as he used one foot to slip the other free of his shoes and then unbuckled his trousers. The kisses continued fervently. His shirt was open and her hands glided over his chest. She heard his heavy cufflinks drop to the ground. Within moments his clothes were littered on the floor beside her dress. He pulled his mouth from hers and his arms scooped her up, her shoes falling from her feet as he carried her into the bedroom. She had one tiny piece of lace clothing on her body and as he lay her on the bed, Ryan slipped that from her too.

There was nothing between them any more. Nothing to stop them from becoming one.

Where the night would lead the next day was irrelevant. Nothing else mattered. Nothing but the hours they were about to share together in that room. In that bed.

With sleepy eyes Molly looked across the crumpled pillow to the man who had spent hours making love to her. The man who had opened her eyes to what she had not known she had been missing before. His hands had caressed her body as if it had been made for him, as if he had read a book written about her, one that told him everything he needed to know.

Ryan pulled Molly gently and purposefully towards him and into his embrace. Her hand instinctively reached across his toned chest as her head rested on his shoulder. He turned his body towards her and his fingers moved the curls falling over her face as he leant in and kissed her.

'I must apologise,' he muttered.

'For what?'

'Not coming good on that drink.'

Molly smiled. 'I think I can forgive your poor hospitality under the circumstances.'

Ryan kissed her again and his hands began trailing over her body. She could feel the urgency in both his kiss and his hands but she became very aware of the time. She had promised to be home by twelve and she was sure it was getting very close to midnight.

She pulled away. 'I would love to continue this all night but I have to go home.'

His hands cupped her face. 'I would love to continue all night too. Are you sure you have to leave?'

'Absolutely… I need to be at home before midnight,' she replied as she sat up, tugging the sheet up with her to cover herself. While she had shared her body with Ryan and shed her inhibitions, she suddenly felt a little vulnerable and self-conscious.

'Of course,' he said. 'I understand.' He sat up with her, pulling her body to his for a moment longer. 'You're a special woman, Molly Murphy. I'm not sure I will be able to sleep alone after lying in this bed with you.'

'I doubt that very much.' She laughed. 'It was quite the workout on your behalf, so I think you'll sleep very well. Even collapse perhaps.'

Ryan kissed her again. 'I met my match, so you should sleep like a log too. The most gorgeous, irresistible log.'

Molly slipped from the bed and raced into the sitting room of the suite to find her dress.

'I'll drive you home,' Ryan called from the bed.

'Don't be silly. You have the room until morning and if Ann is staying with Lizzy you should stay here.'

'No, Molly. I'm not putting you in a cab this late at night.'

Molly felt her heart sink as she heard him walk into the living-room area in search of his own clothes. She didn't turn to face him. She didn't want him to see the worry on her face but equally she didn't want to spoil the night by letting Ryan see where she lived. While she had told him, seeing was quite another matter. It was the wrong side of town and their time together had been more perfect than she could have dreamed possible. It would be the worst ending to the best night of her life.

'Seriously,' she began as she turned to find him doing up his trousers. He was the most perfect man. The best lover and as she looked over at his sculpted chest softly lit she wanted to freeze time and have the night go on for ever. To have him hold her all night long, but she couldn't. She had to get home to Tommy. To her ramshackle home. 'I will slip downstairs and grab a cab from the rank. I'm only ten minutes from the city.'

His frown had eased as he made light of the situation but his eyes had not moved from hers. She suspected there was a serious side to his question. 'I know you live on the wrong side of town, according to you. But is there more to it than that?'

'No...but compared to this...' she looked around the suite '... I'm embarrassed. I don't want you to see the house and feel sorry for me. It's truly dreadful.'

'So, you'd rather hide it from me?'

Molly bit the inside of her cheek and nodded.

'It can't be that bad. Please let me be the judge,' he told her. 'There's one thing you need to know about me, Molly. I can handle almost anything but I don't want anything hidden from me. I'm not sure where we are heading with...this, but wherever this goes, whatever it becomes, it has to be built on honesty.'

Molly took the shoes he held out to her and crossed to the large sofa. She sat down and dropped the shoes on the floor, slipping her feet inside.

With her head facing the ground, she confessed the reason she wanted to catch the cab.

She lifted her eyes to see Ryan's face smiling back at her.

'You don't know how bad. I have no central heating and I live near a train line, a freight-train line. All one hundred and twenty-two carriages pass by twice a day.'

'You count them?'

'Sometimes...'

'If you'll let me, I will gladly take you out more often so you don't have time to count the carriages.'

Molly smiled. 'You might not want to drive over there to pick me up.'

'Molly, some of the coldest people I know live in palatial, centrally heated homes and some of the warmest have no heating at all. And I can safely say that you are the warmest woman I have ever met.'

He walked to her, knelt down on one knee and, cupping her face in his hands, he kissed her. 'I don't give a damn, Molly Murphy, about the suburb, the condition or anything else about your home. As long as there's no man other than your brother living there with you, then there's nothing to hide...but before I take you home, and I am taking you home, I have something for you.'

'What?' she asked, completely taken off guard by the fact he was on one knee. Her curiosity was heading into overdrive as she watched him reach into his pocket.

'You might need these,' he said as he slipped her lace panties into her lap. 'It's cold out tonight.'

Ryan left Molly to stay warm in the room while he walked back down to the convention centre car park and then drove his car back to the hotel. She took only five minutes to tidy her hair and make-up enough to be seen by other guests and then she headed back downstairs. She was barely seated when she saw his midnight-blue sedan pull up and before she could step out he jumped out with the engine running, raced inside, threw his jacket around her shoulders and escorted her back to his car.

'That was very sweet of you but you didn't have to do that. I could have made the dash out to you,' she told him as she secured her seat belt and he did the same.

'I am not going to have you freeze on my watch,' he replied with a kiss before he slipped the car into gear. 'So where exactly do you live?'

'Like I said, I live in a not great part of town but, since you insist, you should take a left at the King William Street lights and I'll guide you from there.'

Ryan winked and Molly couldn't help but

notice on the dashboard clock that it turned midnight as they pulled away from the hotel. And she felt more like Cinderella than she'd thought possible although the idea of Ryan seeing her home still played heavily on her mind.

As they pulled up to her house she noticed Ryan's expression didn't alter. Not at all. Not even a flinch. She'd imagined a look of horror might monopolise his expression as they drove into her suburb and then her street but there was nothing that altered from the time they left the hotel to that moment. No visible change at all. Perhaps again, she thought, she had been the one guilty of judgement. Judging herself and her circumstances more harshly than anyone else. And in the process, judging Ryan.

'This is it, home sweet home,' she said without looking in the direction of the house.

'Molly,' Ryan said. 'Is it normal to have every light on in your house?'

Molly turned to see Ryan was right. The house looked as if a party had started; almost every light had been turned on.

'Oh, dear Lord, Tommy must be up and perhaps looking for me. His anxiety will escalate if he can't find me at this time.'

'Of course,' Ryan said, reaching for his door handle. 'Let me walk you to the door.'

'It's better you don't—it might make it worse. Introductions after midnight won't be good and might make Tommy quite anxious,' she told him, and then leant in and kissed him goodnight. 'Thank you, Ryan, for a wonderful evening.'

'No, thank you, Molly. Truly, one of the best nights in a very long time.'

With that Molly wrapped her thin shawl around her shoulders and alighted the car, not giving Ryan time to open the door for her. She raced to open the rickety gate, then rushed down the path to her front door. She waved to Ryan as she stepped inside. As she closed the door, she heard his car drive off into the night.

She knew he was taking a little piece of her heart with him.

A piece she was very willing to give.

CHAPTER TEN

'ARE YOU ALL RIGHT, Molly? I was very worried.
It's late and the television was off and everything and you weren't here.'

'I'm sorry, Tommy. I was sitting in the car
outside talking to my boss. He drove me home
after the dinner.'

'All right, Molly. But don't worry me again,'
Tommy told her, then left and went back to his
room and closed the door.

Molly felt guilty about worrying Tommy but
had no regrets about the rest of the evening.
Ryan was everything she had been looking for
in a man but had never dreamed even existed
outside a movie or romance novel. He was kind
and considerate…and the most amazing lover,
she added to her mental tally of his praise as
she turned off all the lights, except the night
light in the hallway, and made her way to her
room.

Carefully she slipped out of her dress and

hung it on the hanger behind her door. The care
she took with the gown was at odds with the
way Ryan had discarded it in his eagerness to
have her only hours before. She smiled as she
hurriedly threw pyjamas and woollen socks
on, brushed her teeth and climbed into her
bed. She would deal with her make-up in the
morning. The brushed flannelette sheets were
nothing close to the Egyptian cotton that she
had shared with Ryan but they would quickly
warm up and that was all that was important.
That and reminiscing about the best night of
her life as she drifted off easily into the deep-
est sleep she had enjoyed in more than a year.

Ryan drove into the night thinking about
Molly. She was nothing close to the office
manager he'd had in mind when he'd called the
temp agency and he couldn't have been happier
about that. When he'd asked her to attend the
dinner with him, he had certainly not dreamed
they would end up making love in a hotel suite.
He'd thought he would have a lovely evening
with an intelligent woman. Maybe even learn
a little more about her. Which he had, but it
was so much more than he'd ever expected.

Images of her body filled his mind as he
pulled into his driveway wishing he were not
alone. Wishing she would be in his bed all

night. What had happened between them happened quickly. His feelings had escalated and apparently so had hers. While he certainly had not planned the way the evening had ended, he wouldn't have changed anything about it.

He knew his reputation sat as somewhere between recluse and playboy and he had never bothered to prove anyone wrong. And he realised in many ways perhaps they were right. He was either at home with Lizzy, working or occasionally spending an evening with a woman who wanted nothing more than that one night. No strings attached.

He accepted, although did not agree with, the general consensus that a man who didn't have a permanent partner in his life by close to forty was either somewhat withdrawn or playing the field. Ryan was neither, but he was a father first and foremost and, for good reason, a man who didn't and couldn't trust women, so he didn't feel the need to have someone on his arm. If the opportunity to sleep with an available woman with no expectations of more arose he would accept it, but he didn't go in search of women to fill that void. He had been hurt in the worst possible way and until that night had never met a woman with whom he suddenly felt that there might actually be a reason to open up, to risk being hurt and to want to share his life. He knew it was crazy to feel that way so soon but Molly was so different from anyone he had ever met. She was feisty, yet caring, emotionally intelligent, not to mention beautiful. And the most giving lover.

He wanted her in his life...with strings attached.

He felt himself trusting a woman for the first time in more years than he cared to remember. Against everything he had believed for the longest time, he suddenly realised that he might just have a future with someone. Molly Murphy was an amazing woman and one who could seduce him with the smile in her eyes.

Dr Ryan McFetridge had not noticed the ramshackle houses in the dubious suburb, nor the unsightly graffiti on the run-down buildings near the vacant rail yard, because he had been focussed on the beautiful woman who had captured his heart.

He opened the front door of his home wishing more than anything that he could carry Molly upstairs and hold her in his arms all night long.

Suddenly it hit him. He might just be falling in love.

'Good morning, Molly. I hope Tommy was not too upset that I got you home late.'

'Tommy was a little worried and told me not to be so late again,' Molly said into her phone.

'That was my fault and I take full responsibility.'

'I take equal responsibility. I could have asked to leave the hotel at any time.'

'Well, I hope that you slept well.'

'I slept wonderfully well, in fact I slept in until about twenty minutes ago and didn't even hear the silly side gate that has been banging for the last two nights. When the wind picks up it's like it's possessed.'

'I can come by and fix it if you like.'

'Thank you but there's no need. I called the landlord to do it. He can do something for the rent I give him.'

'Is he on his way over to do it now?'

'God, I hope not. I'm still in my pyjamas.'

'I wish I didn't know that.'

'Why?'

'Because I can imagine how desirable you look…and I want to hold you in my arms again.'

Molly suddenly felt warm all over. The idea was completely impractical but delicious nonetheless. Waking in Ryan's arms would have been the only way to make the night any more perfect than it had been. Ryan was definitely not holding back and playing games. He said it as he felt it, and she loved that level of openness and honesty. He was very different from the closed, guarded man she had first thought him to be.

'I hate to disappoint you but I think the look is more cosy than sexy, to be honest.' Molly brought her thoughts back to reality and confessed as she looked down at her odd socks with lint from the dryer, mismatched pyjamas and oversized dressing gown and screwed up her face. There was nothing sexy about any of it but she didn't have to let on just how bad she looked and spoil his early morning fantasy.

'I'm sure if I was there I would disagree,' he told her, then continued. 'I know it's early to be calling and I do apologise but I wondered if you and Tommy would like to go on a picnic. It's cold today but not going to rain so I thought we could rug up and head up to Waterfall Gully. I could swing by and pick you up at about noon. I thought if I give you plenty of warning then it's more likely to be a yes.'

Molly chuckled at his line of thinking. It was considerate, and also not hiding his intentions. As Ryan had already seen her home and still wanted to venture back into the suburb, she was not about to decline but she had to consider Tommy's view of the invitation as she had already left him alone the night before

and wanted him to be happy about the outing. 'That sounds wonderful but I will have
to check with Tommy and get back to you,'
Molly told her early morning caller. 'Is Lizzy
up to coming?'

'No, she's still not good. It's usually two
days before she's feeling up to doing much but
Ann's here with her for the day. I told her what
I had in mind and Lizzy's actually encouraging me to go out with you. She really likes you,
Molly. To be honest, if it wasn't for me knowing that she really was unwell last night, I'd
think she set the whole thing up. Looks like
she's dabbling in a bit of matchmaking.'

'I'm not sure about that but I think Lizzy's
a very special young lady.'

'I'd have to agree with you,' he replied before returning to his original question. 'Please
ask Tommy if he's up to it. And take as long as
you need. I've packed the picnic lunch already
with enough for the three of us so just let me
know by, say…eleven-thirty.'

'I will have an answer for you before then,
and thank you, Ryan, for the invitation, and
thank you for including Tommy.'

'You're very welcome and of course I
would include Tommy. I'm looking forward
to meeting him and, since Lizzy doesn't have
a brother, it might be nice for them to hang out

in the future too. There's not a big age difference so they might become famous friends.'

'That would be great. I'll get back to you as soon as I know.'

Molly hung up with her heart as light as air. She didn't think anything could wipe the smile from her face. Thinking way too far ahead, Molly wishfully thought they had the potential to be like the Brady Bunch with Tommy and Lizzy and Ryan and herself. Could it be possible that she and Ryan could be more than just a fling? She had never thought she would learn to trust a man again, let alone contemplate falling in love, but that was exactly what was happening to her and she wanted to rest back and enjoy the feeling.

Could Ryan be her happily ever after and a stable male figure for Tommy? He had an understanding of the special needs of a young man like Tommy as he was successfully raising Lizzy and, to the best of her knowledge, coping with those challenges. She was daydreaming and in bliss as she walked past Tommy's door that was still shut. He too must be sleeping in, she thought, and she gathered her things to have a shower.

The warm water felt wonderful running all over her body but not as good as Ryan's hands the night before. The heat in the steam-filled room was heavenly on a cold morning but Ryan's fingers had been ecstasy. Life had certainly turned the corner for her and Tommy. Perhaps, she mused for a moment as she lathered her hands with the cake of soap, both Murphys might be lucky in love after all.

'Tommy, are you on the telephone?'

'I was but I'm not now. My girlfriend had to go,' Tommy called from behind his closed door. His voice told Molly he was grumpy.

'Well, it's lovely that you can call her and talk,' she replied, hoping to lift his spirits. 'She must be very special because I know you like her very much.'

'I love her.'

Molly quickly took stock of her words and her attitude. She kept forgetting that Tommy was a twenty-five-year-old man in love.

'Of course, you do. Do you have plans today or would you like to come on a picnic?'

'No. I want to stay at home.'

'May I come in, Tommy? It's difficult to have a conversation with your door closed.'

'Yes. You can open the door.'

Molly slowly opened the door to find her brother sitting on his bed. His head was hanging down and he looked very forlorn. 'I thought you might like to go out and have a picnic,'

Molly said, still hoping to cheer him up with the idea of an outing. 'Ryan asked us both out for the day.'

'He's your boss.'

'That's right.'

'He took you out to dinner.'

'Yes, he did and we had a lovely time.'

'You came home late and made me worry.'

Molly chewed the inside of her cheek for a moment. She was slap bang in the middle of a grilling from her baby brother. 'I know I did.'

'Do you like him?'

'He's very nice.'

'Is he your boyfriend?'

Molly was taken aback by the line of questioning. It was unlike Tommy. She could see he wasn't happy and she wasn't sure about the answer to his last question. Was Ryan her boyfriend? She didn't know herself. The fact he had called so early and planned a date for the three of them could lead her to assume they were dating but she wasn't sure and she wasn't ready to tell Tommy anything until she was sure.

'Tommy, Ryan is a friend and a very nice man and I think you would like him.'

'I was going to see my girlfriend today but I can't. She's staying home. I wanted to go to the mall and get a ring and then ask her to marry me.'

Molly almost dropped her coffee cup and some colourful language with the shock. She knew that Tommy had spoken of a girlfriend but had assumed it was a fleeting crush. He had a big heart and it had been filled with romantic thoughts about pretty girls before but after a few weeks he usually found the girls to be silly and he stopped talking about them. She had suspected this wouldn't be any different but it clearly was very different. Molly doubted Tommy had ever kissed or been kissed. His crushes had been platonic and innocent up to that point.

Molly's head had been in the clouds with her own romantic thoughts and she had forgotten to enquire further about Tommy's girlfriend, but talk of marriage was the last thing she'd expected to hear from her little brother.

'She's so pretty and we've worked together for over a year. I was her boss for a few weeks but now she's a boss like me. I have four people who work for me folding the mail and she has three. She started there on May the second last year. I remember because it was her birthday the next day,' he continued happily, completely unaware of the panic washing over his sister.

'And you want to get married?'

'Yes, and I want to buy a ring. A pretty one that she will like so she says yes to me.'

Molly steadied her breathing so her brother didn't notice her reaction. Everyone deserved to find someone to love and she didn't want her brother to think he deserved anything less but she couldn't help but be surprised and apprehensive. It was all happening so very fast. The week before she hadn't known Tommy had a girl in his life and now he wanted to get married. It was a lot to absorb. And she needed to know he was sure about his feelings before he got too involved.

Suddenly she pulled herself up. Her relationship with Ryan had moved even more quickly. She had met, fallen in love and slept with a man she had known for only a week. It was against everything she had thought she would have done. In fact, she'd never thought she would get that close to a man again, let alone in seven days.

'Do you want to come and sit on the sofa with me? I can put on the heater and we can chat. I want you to tell me everything about her,' Molly said as she headed in the direction of the living room. She needed to give her complete attention to her brother as this was a life-changing decision he was about to make. She turned on the gas heater and closed the door to keep the heat in the room, then dropped to the floor and sat cross-legged with her coffee cup in her hand. She could hear the side gate banging again against the wrought-iron fence in the strong wind. Molly had tied it up so many times but it always came free. She made a mental note to put one of the broken red house bricks on either side once the rain stopped. The thought of going outside and getting wet through once again that week was worse than the incessant and annoying noise. They were snug and warm inside and there were so many questions Molly had for Tommy, but she wanted to take it slowly.

'Honey is like the prettiest flower in the garden, only better,' he said, holding his arms out wide with a smile to match. 'She's the prettiest girl in the world and if she says yes then we'll get married.'

'Do you think she knows you're going to ask her?'

'No, but we love each other. I told her that I love her and she told me that she loves me.'

'I know you've worked together for over a year but how long have you been together as boyfriend and girlfriend?'

'Six weeks.'

'I see, and how old is she?'

'She's young. She doesn't have wrinkles like the lady that drives the bus.'

Molly was glad to hear that, since the bus driver was a retired volunteer in her early seventies.

'Do you think you might like to get to know each other for a little bit longer before you get married?'

'Do you think she will say no?' Tommy's face suddenly became overcome with sadness.

Molly couldn't bear to think she had made her brother sad. Not for even a second.

'I'm sure she will say yes. She would be lucky to be married to you. It's just…' Molly hesitated, not wanting to say anything that would create doubt in Tommy's heart about how Honey felt about him, but she did have some reservations. 'It's just that I'd like to meet her too. And maybe her parents, and you don't have to rush. You might like to take things slowly. It takes time to know that you are really in love,' Molly said, and immediately felt like the world's biggest hypocrite. She was telling her brother to take things slowly and she definitely had not. Clearly she wasn't listening to her own advice. Never had there been a better case of *Do as I say, not as I do*. She didn't want to have two sets of rules and hated that her first reaction was to do just that. It wasn't right but she was so accustomed to being protective and she was struggling to step away from that role and feel the same level of excitement that her brother felt.

But she had to do just that. She knew in her heart that she had to be happy for Tommy. No matter what the future held, she needed to push away her reservations and doubt and find happiness for him. Real happiness. He needed to know that she was sharing his joy.

Tommy tilted his head a little. 'You mean sleepovers? Like Nigel did?'

Molly almost choked on her warm drink. She hadn't been expecting to hear that. Being reminded that Nigel had slept in her bed was upsetting and equally the thought of her little brother having a young woman in his bed would take a little getting accustomed to by Molly. Marriage, sleepovers, all of it had been sudden and she was struggling to know how to feel about it.

'You will like her, Molly. She's neat.'

Molly smiled. She loved her brother and she would support him however she could, but she knew there could be challenges ahead for him and his future bride if he was to marry his girlfriend. 'I know I will like her very, very much.'

'Can she come for dinner one night?' Tommy

asked, smoothing down his hair as if his pro-spective bride were in the room.

'Of course, she can. I told you that I would love to meet her.'

'You promise, she can come over.'

'Definitely.'

'All right, but it can't be today. She can't see me today but she still loves me.'

Molly could see the potential for heartbreak but she could also see the potential for love and she was well aware she couldn't influence the outcome. Just be there to support the one she loved no matter what. She was yet to meet the young woman who had claimed her brother's heart. While he was sensible and relatively in-dependent, Molly still wanted to ensure that this young woman had his best interests as well as her own in mind.

The guilt she felt in losing the family home played heavily as well. Tommy wouldn't have very much to offer his bride-to-be and the sheer practicality of getting a home would be difficult. Fortunately, there was some insur-ance money still in trust for Tommy that would be accessible to him when he turned thirty, not sufficient to buy a big home, but he could purchase a modest home in a nice suburb. But that was more than five years away and she wasn't sure his bride-to-be would be happy waiting that long.

Her mood became sombre for a moment as she looked out of the window and thought back to what she had done. A wolf in sheep's clothing had come knocking on her door and she had let him in. Taken him at his word and allowed him to become part of the family and with that allowed her financial security to be exposed and put at risk. Suddenly she worried if she had done the same in trusting Ryan. Was it too soon to really know him? Should she have waited before falling into bed and potentially into love with her boss?

She tried to push her negative thoughts aside and remind herself that Ryan was in a different league. He was the kindest, most chivalrous man she had met. She wanted the doubt to disappear, her fears to leave, but there were traces and, while she suspected they might always be there lurking in her mind, she couldn't and wouldn't allow her past to cripple her future. Ryan McFetridge was not like Nigel and never would be. He was not the type of man who would pull the rug out from under her. She hoped with all of her heart that Dr McFetridge was there to stay…no matter what.

'What if we have the picnic lunch together

and then go with you to the mall and pick out a ring?'

'With your boyfriend?'

Molly ran her fingers through the unruly curls as she wondered how to answer her brother. She decided to brush over the reference to boyfriend. 'We could ask Ryan if he would like to come along, but only if you want that.'

'Maybe. What will we have for lunch?'

'Something delicious, I'm sure.'

Molly smiled. Tommy was bending to the idea. She wanted so much for Ryan and Tommy to meet and then Tommy and Lizzy to meet. For the first time in a long time she thought she might only be a few steps away from her happy ever after.

Ryan came exactly on noon and Molly and Tommy were ready and waiting by the door. It was cold outside but the sun was shining and the sky was the most vivid blue. They were rugged up with scarves and gloves and winter coats, and Molly thought it would be lovely to be out in the fresh air. Particularly with her two favourite men.

'Hi, Ryan, please come inside,' Molly said as she opened the front door to her tiny home. She kissed him on the cheek, mindful that she hadn't confirmed to Tommy the status of her relationship with Ryan yet and she didn't want to rush anything in front of her brother. Ryan gave her a knowing smile that told her immediately he understood how the day would play out for the three of them.

'Tommy, this is Ryan McFetridge,' she began the introductions as soon as Ryan stepped inside. 'Ryan, this is my brother, Tommy.'

Ryan extended his hand and Tommy chose not to meet his handshake. Neither Molly nor Ryan said anything and quietly accepted that Tommy was not yet ready to greet him favourably. Molly hoped that would change in time but understood, after losing Nigel abruptly, that he would be hesitant to get close to Ryan in a hurry. Tommy had liked Nigel. Why wouldn't he? He had said and done everything to make Tommy like and trust him all the while stealing his inheritance. This time they needed to take things slowly so Tommy could really get to know Ryan and feel safe.

They needed to take things a day at a time and see if this was a for-ever relationship. While it seemed wonderful, Molly knew there was another person to consider in any decisions she made about seriously dating Ryan.

'If you're ready, I have the heaters on in the car and we can head up and have a picnic.'

'Okay,' Tommy answered matter-of-factly, and stepped outside to see a shiny red SUV at the front of the house. Suddenly his face lit up. 'That's a neat car.'

'Glad you like it,' Ryan replied. 'It's our weekend car. We like to get out for long drives and head into the hills and, when I get holidays, we go to the Flinders Ranges to stay. My daughter chose the car. She loves the colour red.'

'Me too.'

Molly was surprised to hear Tommy say that. She didn't know he liked red. She'd thought blue had been his favourite colour for a very long time. But she was just happy to see her brother happy so didn't question his new colour preference.

Tommy climbed into the back while Ryan opened the car door for Molly. She was relieved to see a level of enthusiasm from her brother.

'You have a DVD screen,' Tommy said gleefully before Ryan closed Molly's door.

'Yes, Tommy. I'll start it for you as soon as I get in.'

Ryan kept his word and the moment he was seated inside the car, he lowered the ceiling screen. 'I have a few DVDs here or a cable so you can stream from your smartphone.'

'I don't have a smartphone,' Tommy told him bluntly. 'Smartphones cost too much money so Molly and I don't have one.'

'I agree. I just have one because I'm on call,' Ryan replied. 'But don't worry, you can stream from mine. Let's get you set up before we head off.'

Molly watched as Ryan did just that. Tommy chose a science fiction movie he wanted to see even though the trip was only thirty minutes, and the three of them headed off for their picnic. Molly was so happy to be spending time with Ryan, and having Tommy along with them made it a perfect day.

The picnic lunch was wonderful. There were wooden tables and benches in the small park at the foot of the gully climbing trail. Ryan had packed everything they would need, right down to a checked tablecloth and thick woollen blankets to throw over their legs. There were two home-made salads, one was pasta and the other Greek with feta cheese and olives, a loaf of fresh crusty bread, bottled water, a still-warm rotisserie chicken that Ryan didn't take credit for as his local chicken shop did better than he could by a mile, and roast potatoes, again courtesy of Charlie's Chickens on Portrush Road.

They all tucked into the food and, once it was finished, they enjoyed piping hot chocolate from a flask.

'That was good, Ryan,' Tommy said, pulling the serviette free from his collar. Then he turned to Molly. 'Can I make a call to my girlfriend?'

'Sure,' Molly said.

'If you'd like privacy, you can make the call in my car, Tommy. Here's the keys,' Ryan added, pulling the keys from his coat pocket and handing them to Tommy. 'The top button on the remote unlocks the doors.'

Tommy nodded, took the keys and headed to the car only twenty metres away in the almost empty car park.

'Thank you for that,' Molly said, squeezing Ryan's hand under the table and out of view of Tommy. 'That was very sweet of you.'

'He's a grown man. I think he deserves privacy,' Ryan reasoned.

'Sometimes I forget that. I try to make sure I don't treat him differently, but when he told me this morning that he's going to ask his girlfriend, Honey, to marry him, I have to admit it freaked me out. He's twenty-five but I still think of him as my little brother.'

'Wow, marriage. I can see it would. Marriage is a big step. Have they been together for a long time?'

'Six weeks, but apparently worked together for a year.'

'That's moving fast but sometimes you just know.'

Molly felt her heart race yet again with the way he looked at her as he spoke. She wondered if that was how he felt about her.

'Have you met this mystery young woman?' he finally said.

'No.' She was shaking her head. 'Which is making me a little anxious. I'm sure she's lovely but I don't know anything about her. Tommy's been waiting for that special someone and he always spoke about getting married and settling down. I guess I never thought it would really happen.'

'Well, I think you need to get to know the young woman and her family before the lovebirds set a date. There's lots for everyone to think about, but if they're in love then you may not be able to stop them becoming engaged and it's not your place to try,' Ryan remarked, then, looking over to Tommy chatting happily in the car, added, 'But you can make sure there's plenty of time between the engagement and the wedding so they don't rush into anything that they're not ready for.'

'Let's hope I can stall them. On that subject, Tommy would like to go to the mall later. I've suggested the Eastern Hills Mall as it's open until late tonight with the mid-winter sales.'

'Would you like me to accompany you or is this brother-sister time?'

'If you don't mind, it would be lovely for you to go with us. Perhaps a man's opinion would help. He actually wants to buy the engagement ring today.'

Ryan ran his fingers across his forehead. 'He's not wasting any time. He's a man on a mission.'

'Apparently.'

'If he'd like me to be there, I'm happy to do so. Does he have a budget? The jewellery shops in the Eastern Hills Mall are quite pricey.'

'He's been saving hard and now wants to spend it all on the ring.'

'She must be quite the catch.'

'Honey is apparently *a princess*,' she said.

'Then I'm sure I can help to haggle a little. Even in those stores there's room to move on prices.'

Molly looked into the warmest, most caring eyes and wanted so badly to kiss the man sitting beside her. He was so wonderful and understanding. A true knight in shining armour who made the best pasta salad she had ever

eaten. She could see Tommy in the car glancing up at them now and then, so she refrained
from acting on her impulse. She didn't want
to surprise Tommy by making it obvious Ryan
was more to her than a friend too soon.

But with little effort Ryan was becoming
more and more to her with every passing minute they shared.

And the winter picnic was no exception.

CHAPTER ELEVEN

RYAN DID JUST as he promised and managed to have the price reduced on the very pretty ring so it came in under Tommy's budget. While the diamond was quite tiny, the white-gold setting was pretty and Tommy particularly liked the red velvet box.

The three of them then headed to Molly's home. Molly had suggested Ryan stay for dinner and Tommy seemed keen on the idea too, but Ryan declined as he wanted to check in on Lizzy.

As they pulled up in front of their home, Ryan turned in his seat. 'Good luck with the proposal, Tommy.'

'Thank you, Ryan. I'm going to work hard and save my money and buy a house so we can be happy. And you can live with us too, Molly, so you won't be alone.'

Ryan shot a sideways smile at Molly.

'You're a good man, Tommy, and any girl would be lucky to have you.'

Molly and Tommy ate dinner together and, after the dishes were washed and put away, Tommy went to his room leaving Molly alone with her thoughts. He was tired and also excited. He told her he would guard the ring with his life until he proposed.

Molly hugged him goodnight and sat by the heater. Her week had certainly been monumental, she thought as she stretched her pyjama-clad legs out in front of her and rested her head on the sofa. Closing her eyes, she thought back over the previous seven days. She had started a new job, received a pay rise, attended a black-tie dinner with her boss in the most gorgeous new dress, they'd made love, had gone on a second, picnic date…and she accepted that she had fallen for him. A week ago, she could never have imagined her life turning around like that.

She had paid her rent, health insurance and they'd enjoyed salmon for dinner. She hoped it was not too good to be true and the bubble burst but she couldn't see how it would. Common sense was telling her to tread carefully but her heart and gut were urging her to throw caution to the wind and enjoy the happiness the universe was gifting to her. While an argument raged in her head between logic and emotions, with emotions the favourite to win, she was startled by a dragging sound outside. She stood to investigate. Pulling back the drapes, she saw a figure outside holding the side gate in place with his foot while he put bricks on either side. Her stomach dropped. She couldn't make out his face as he was hunched trying to sort out the loose gate but she suspected it was the landlord's son. She shuddered at the thought of him coming to her home late in the evening. What was he hoping to achieve? She had already told him she was not interested in him and the rent was fully paid. She suddenly remembered when she paid the rent she had told him that the gate was banging all night and she wanted it fixed. She'd meant in the day when she wasn't at home, not late in the evening.

She peered into the darkness and as the stranger turned his head under the dim street light she realised it was Ryan.

She rushed to the door and then mid-step realised she was wearing her pyjamas.

Suddenly she didn't care. She was curious as to why he was back there but excited to see him and her state of dress didn't matter.

'Ryan,' she called out from the open front door. 'What are you doing out there?'

'Stopping your side gate from banging all night and keeping you awake. I remembered when I got home that I had wanted to sort it out so I'll do that and leave…'

'Are you serious?'

'Absolutely not. I'm hoping to come inside. I brought a bottle of wine and some chocolate-dipped strawberries that Ann made with Lizzy today. I thought we could spend the evening together since Tommy already knows about me. I hoped it would be okay.'

A little while later, with Molly still in her flannelette pyjamas, the two of them sat side by side on the floor by the heater in her tiny lounge. Tommy had stepped out of his room to get a glass of milk, said hello to Ryan, took two strawberries and then headed back into his room. Molly was pleasantly surprised at how quickly he had accepted Ryan in their home almost like a piece of furniture. The day together and Ryan's help in finding a ring for Tommy's soon-to-be fiancée had made all the difference. Ryan's support had been unconditional even though Molly knew he had a few reservations about the proposal and the marriage. But for Tommy's sake, he kept that to himself.

Molly sipped her wine and leant back into Ryan's arms as she nibbled on the very ripe strawberry coated in the darkest Swiss chocolate. It had been for ever since she had enjoyed a glass of wine in her own home or such a delicious fruit treat. It was a luxury her situation had not afforded but, she conceded silently, being in the arms of Ryan would have made vinegar taste like champagne. They were facing the television but it wasn't turned on.

'I have to say, Molly, after everything you told me last night, I think you're even more amazing.'

Molly shook her head.

'I mean it—you are so strong. Others might have crumbled with the disappointment of being left and the struggle that followed but you chose to fight on.'

'Everything I did, I did for Tommy. I could never walk away from him.'

'And when you came to work for me, despite what you were going through, you found a way to make improvements to the running of my practice.'

'Clearly I wasn't doing that well… I turned up looking like I'd been caught in a monsoon, not to mention the odd shoes…'

'But you turned up to a job that was not using your skills and well beneath your pay grade to put food on the table and be here at home at the right time to keep Tommy feeling secure. Some women walk away from anything that hard. And they feel nothing for those left empty and hurt by their actions.'

Molly turned her face towards Ryan. The conversation had taken a detour to a place that confused her. It was a side of him that seemed quite dark. 'That sounds like you're speaking from experience.'

'You're more than just a pretty face...'

Molly brushed aside the joke he tried to use to cover up his feelings. 'I'm serious, Ryan. What happened to you?'

Ryan drew a deep breath and pulled away slightly from Molly. She could feel him retreating but knew he needed the space.

'You know Lizzy's my daughter but what you don't know is that I only found out that I had a daughter seven years ago. Lizzy was twelve when I discovered I was her father.'

'Lizzy was twelve before you knew?' Molly asked, her confusion at his announcement not hidden.

'I only found out that I had a daughter when her adoptive parents both passed away within three months of each other. They say that her adoptive mother had a stroke and passed, and her adoptive father died of a broken heart.'

'You must have been quite young when she was born.'

'Two months short of twenty. Lizzy was born on the third of May and I was born on July third but I didn't find out until I was almost thirty-two. I dated a girl, Madeline, in my hometown of Port Lincoln and we broke up when I was nineteen. We'd started going out in high school and dated for close to three years. I would travel back every few weeks from Adelaide where I was in my first year of medicine and call every day but it wasn't enough. She didn't like the long-distance relationship and I wasn't prepared to throw in my studies to live in a tiny town and work for her father's prawn-trawling business. We came to a stalemate and she gave me an ultimatum that I needed to move back home and marry her or she would end it. She was calling my bluff, thinking I would move back, but I was young and decided I needed to stay in Adelaide, finish my studies and think about marriage down the track. We broke up. It was inevitable when two people can't compromise. We were too young to really understand what compromise even meant.'

'Even though you were young, it still must have hurt. Three years is a long time.'

'It was hard for a while, but again I was so

young and my focus was on getting my medical degree and then deciding where I wanted to live. Maybe it would be a country doctor, but I hadn't lived anywhere but Port Lincoln so I wanted to spread my wings before I nested.'

'That was a sensible idea. Nineteen is so very young to get married and settle down for life.'

'She clearly didn't think so,' Ryan said, glancing back at Molly and then back to the black television screen. 'It was about three months after we ended it, Madeline discovered she was pregnant. She decided not to tell me as she was already seeing a local lad and she decided that he would probably marry her and they could live happily ever after with no one the wiser.'

'Three months…then could the other young man have been the baby's father.'

'No, they had only been seeing each other for about six weeks and as she'd irregular periods she hadn't paid much attention to being late. She thought it must have been the upset of the break-up and teenage hormones and we'd always been careful, as much as teenagers could be, so she had no reason to think she was pregnant, but the doctor told her she was already close to three months. So, she decided it was going to be her secret.'

'But how did she think she could keep that kind of secret?'

'She planned on telling everyone the baby was premature.'

Molly was shocked by the level of deception at such a young age. 'But that's wrong in so many ways.'

'She was young, angry with me and wanted to get married and settle down and thought that the baby would cement things with her new boyfriend. She was scared I wouldn't come back to live there and she'd be raising the baby alone.'

'I'm sure she was wrong. Even only knowing you for a week, I think you would have done the right thing.'

'I've thought about that over the years, and I say now that I would but I can't say with any certainty what I would have done at nineteen. Perhaps I would have married her, perhaps not, but I know that I would've taken care of my child financially.'

'I don't believe for a moment that, at nineteen or any age, you would have left her to raise the baby alone.'

'I appreciate your belief in me,' he told her and, pulling her close, he kissed the top of her head.

'How could I not believe in you? I've seen

how much you love Lizzy. You would give her the world if you could and I doubt that's just because you're older and wiser. I think it's because of who you are as a man. And the way you relate to Tommy after only just meeting him.'

Ryan said nothing but Molly could see the past was preoccupying his thoughts. She drew her legs up underneath her body as she faced him.

'If you don't mind me asking, how did her new boyfriend take the news of the baby?'

'He apparently was surprised, very surprised, but at Madeline's request her father offered him a job with the family business and he took it. He was a local farmhand so it was a step up for him. They planned on getting married after the baby was born. She wanted her figure back to walk down the aisle and felt secure, with the new boyfriend on the payroll and a baby on the way, that he wouldn't leave her.'

'But didn't she worry the baby wouldn't look like her boyfriend?'

'She had a type. He pretty much had my height and colouring. It seemed like a flawless plan to her.'

Molly was stunned by everything she was hearing. For a teenager to be so calculating and cover all her bases to get the outcome she wanted disturbed Molly. She also worried how Madeline's personality had evolved over the years. She hoped she might have looked inside and discovered a moral compass but she had her doubts.

'Unfortunately for Madeline, it didn't work out the way it was planned,' Ryan continued. 'Elizabeth was born on her due date and with Down's syndrome. The young man then made enquiries with the doctor if the prematurity had anything to do with Lizzy's condition and the doctor told him that Lizzy had been born on the date she was expected.'

'She didn't have antenatal check-ups and discover Lizzy's condition before she was born?'

'The chances of Down's syndrome in a woman under thirty are about one in twelve hundred and there was no one in the family with the condition so no one thought that would be a consideration that justified the testing.'

'So, what happened?'

'Well, the relationship went south after he discovered she had been lying to him. He left Madeline and the family business. Her father was close to disowning her for lying to everyone as they were good people. They quickly realised it was my baby.'

'Did they contact you?'

'I wish they had but they didn't. They put Lizzy up for adoption. The couple who adopted Lizzy were a couple in the country. They were childless and in their late forties. Bob and Laura Jones knew Lizzy would have special needs but Laura had nursing experience and they were prepared to provide her with whatever she needed and more. Madeline's mother, Ann, had wanted to raise the baby but her husband, while a good man, was practical and said it was not in anyone's best interest to hold on to Lizzy. He said it was too much to take on. Their daughter's life had fallen apart after the lies were exposed and Madeline wanted nothing to do with the child, so Ann had no choice but to agree that the baby be put up for private adoption.'

'Ann who's now called Sooty?'

'Yes, one and the same. She would send birthday and Christmas presents along with money to the agency to be forwarded on. The adoptive parents were not wealthy and they accepted the gifts on behalf of their daughter. Ann felt it would be disruptive to meet Lizzy so she never asked for the new parents' details, but she left hers if they ever asked for them. While it was a strange relationship, it allowed Ann to keep her sanity and Bob and Laura

Jones had the additional financial assistance to raise their much-loved daughter.'

'So that is why Lizzy's surname is Jones.'

'Yes. I didn't change it when she came to live with me. By twelve, she had learnt her name. While coming to live with me brought a lot of challenges, as you could certainly well understand, changing her name would have been very confusing and unnecessary.'

'What happened after her adoptive parents died, before she came to live with you?'

'Ann received a letter from the agency telling her that Bob had passed a few months after his wife.'

'That's so sad. And poor Lizzy.'

'Well, Lizzy had been taken in by the neighbours but they were unable to offer her a home long-term as they had five children of their own. They offered a month so a new family could be found to adopt or foster Lizzy. This broke Ann's heart and she didn't want Lizzy to ever live in foster care. She genuinely loved the child she had never met but her circumstances had changed. In the twelve years since Lizzy was born, her husband had died and she was getting older and worried if something happened to her then Lizzy might once again be facing fostering.

'If she had been ten years younger, I know

she would have taken Lizzy into her home. Anyway, in desperation she reached out to me. She tracked me down through networks on the Eyre Peninsula who knew where I was practising in Adelaide. I received a call out of the blue asking if I could travel to Port Lincoln urgently. While I had no clue what to think, I flew over there. I thought perhaps something had happened to Madeline, but I quickly found out that she had long moved away and forgotten everyone and everything that had been a part of her life in Port Lincoln. Ann poured out everything to me.'

'That must have been such a shock for you. Trying to absorb everything at once. I can't imagine what you went through that day.'

'It was devastating in so many ways and I felt so many emotions that day. A bit like I had been run over by a bus. Twelve years of deceit came undone and I felt enormous pressure, as if I was just supposed to ride in and sort it out. I left Ann's home not sure what to think or do. I was angry beyond belief, and hurt and disappointed, but the next day the concern I had for the daughter I never knew became the strongest emotion and driving force behind my decision. I called the agency, undertook a paternity test to prove I was Lizzy's father to the authorities and began the process of bringing Lizzy to live with me.'

Molly did not know how to react, except to reach for Ryan's hand and gently squeeze it. He didn't pull away.

'I guess the rest is history and I have spent the last seven years getting to know Lizzy. I struggle every day with the years I lost, the years I was shut out of Lizzy's life, and for that I guess it's no surprise that I have little time for anyone who's not upfront with me. I can deal with anything, bad news, horrific news, but not secrets. It does my head in.'

'And Lizzy's mother?'

'Last I heard she's living in the US, married to a marine she met while he was on shore leave in Australia and they have three boys. Sending Lizzy to live over there would have been wrong on so many levels, including the fact the life of a military family has no stability and we both know that a child with Down's syndrome needs routine. Quite apart from the fact that Madeline didn't want her daughter.'

'How can a mother not want her own child?'

'Apparently, it was relatively easy for Madeline,' Ryan said, shrugging his shoulders. 'But I have to admit the disaster she left behind wasn't easy for anyone. It was a daily challenge for Lizzy to settle with me but we worked very hard over a long time and Ann helped when I finally let her back into our lives. She felt guilty for not reaching out to me, but to be honest, with all the deception from their daughter, neither Ann nor her husband had been thinking clearly. He'd just wanted what was best for Lizzy and I think to have the scandal fade away by Lizzy not being there. And Ann knew their daughter was not the type to provide the care that Lizzy needed. And they were right.'

'What do you mean by "finally let her back into our lives"?'

'I blamed her for the longest time. About a year, actually. I didn't respond to her calls or emails after Lizzy came to live with me. I told the agency to return any gifts that were sent to them and I returned anything sent to my practice. I wanted to punish someone for what had happened and I couldn't punish Madeline or Madeline's father so I took it out on Ann. In hindsight, it wasn't fair but Lizzy didn't know her grandmother and at the time I was not thinking logically.'

Molly feared her judgement of his actions would be evident on her face but she couldn't prevent it. It was understandable but still harsh.

'I finally realised that I was punishing the wrong person. If she hadn't kept in contact with Lizzy's adoptive family over the years, and also reached out to me and risked my wrath, then Lizzy would be God knows where now. It just took me a while to accept that I needed to let go of the blame and move forward, so I reached out and apologised for what I then saw as cruel. Ann had no family in Port Lincoln as Madeline was in the US and Ann's husband was gone, so I suggested she move down to Adelaide so she could be closer to Lizzy and myself.'

'Well, that was pretty wonderful of you.'

'I don't know about wonderful, but I thought it was the right thing to do. We all needed each other. And I wanted her to finally get to know her granddaughter. Now Ann is a patient at the practice and for her age has very little to be worried about. She's in great health.'

'I don't know what to say. It's an incredible story…with a happy ending.'

'It's better than it could have been, but not as good as it should have been if everyone had just told the truth nineteen years ago. We've all come through it, but I can't say unscathed and it could have been avoided.'

Molly had never expected Ryan to talk about his past to her so openly and honestly. She had never met a man so willing to share his thoughts and his experiences, good and bad. Each word brought him closer to her.

But it also cast a dark shadow over the two of them.

Sitting there holding the hand of a man who had been deceived by so many, she suddenly realised that she might be doing the same. While she had not taken Lizzy's secret boyfriend too seriously at the time, knowing now how Ryan felt about his daughter dating, would he find her silence on the matter as betrayal? But if she came clean about it, then she would be breaking her promise to Lizzy.

And could she ever win Lizzy's trust again?

Molly sat wrapped in the warmth of a wonderful man's embrace, silently debating her options. She quickly realised they were limited. She had to pray Lizzy's infatuation ended quickly and, when it did, swear to herself that she would never again make a promise she couldn't keep.

Because she knew in keeping her promise to Lizzy she might be taking a huge risk in having a future with Ryan.

CHAPTER TWELVE

I<small>T WAS</small> S<small>ATURDAY</small> morning and the weather had eased a little with no rain scheduled for the day. The breeze was still bitter and the dark clouds hung low in the sky like a dull canvas. Molly wasn't sure if the bureau of meteorology had it right or not, but she dressed in jeans and a sweater.

She wasn't planning to go out until late in the day so it didn't much matter what was happening outside. There was so much happening inside her own head she would deal with rain if and when it eventuated. Molly had just cooked a hearty breakfast of bacon and eggs to share with Tommy. It was a Saturday morning ritual to relax and eat a nice breakfast because the rest of the week they would be rushing to get to work.

Molly had not seen Ryan outside the practice all week as he had late-night rounds and spent three evenings consulting at St Clara's, but the time they spent at work he did not hide his feelings for her. When they were alone at the end of the day, he pulled her close and his kisses were as passionate as the night they'd spent together. She melted in his arms and couldn't wait to spend another night in his bed. But they were both very professional in front of patients and his nurse Stacy when she was rostered on. Molly liked Stacy but they were both so busy they didn't have much time for social chit-chat, which was probably for the best because Molly didn't like her chances of hiding how she felt about Ryan if questioned by her colleague.

They'd made plans to have dinner that night. Ryan was going to pick Molly up at seven o'clock. He had asked her out on the Monday morning, so with plenty of notice she had managed to find a lovely little black dress on sale at a department store in town. She would wear the same nude patent shoes and bag. And while she wanted to look nice, she wasn't stressing about impressing him—he had seen her in her flannelette pyjamas and hadn't bolted so she felt a little more secure about her appearance.

But while she was excited and so looking forward to being alone with Ryan again, Molly felt torn between keeping Lizzy's confidence and being honest and open with Ryan. She made a promise to herself that she would give

Lizzy one week to tell her father. After that she would have to take it into her own hands. She wasn't entirely sure how she would manage the situation but she would find a way.

Molly served breakfast and called out to Tommy. He came quickly to the table and was wearing a big smile.

'You look happy this morning.'

'Because I am happy… Lizzy said yes. She will marry me.'

'Lizzy?'

'My girlfriend, Lizzy.'

'But your girlfriend's name is Honey.'

Tommy laughed as he tucked his serviette into the neck of his jumper and reached for his knife and fork. 'I call her Honey. She calls me Sweetheart. Her name is Lizzy. We sat under the trees yesterday. I asked her to marry me and she said yes and she kissed me and I kissed her back.'

'Oh, my God, I had no idea her name was Lizzy…' Molly dropped her own fork and stopped mid-sentence. She was aware of the sudden shrill tone to her voice and needed to calm down. She didn't want to upset Tommy, who was clearly thrilled his proposal had been accepted. She also reminded herself that Lizzy was not an unusual name.

'I told you,' he said, before he took another mouthful of the scrambled eggs.

'No, Tommy, I would have remembered.'

'Are you cross, Molly?'

'No, not with you. Not at all. It was my fault I didn't ask,' she said, patting his hand over the breakfast table. Molly wondered why she had never questioned Tommy more about his girlfriend before that day. She'd had a lot on her mind and Tommy had called her *Honey* and Molly had thought that was her name. Not her pet name. Everything had been travelling at lightning speed the previous week and Molly hadn't read between the lines.

And clearly Ryan hadn't doubted that Honey was Tommy's girlfriend's name when they'd all shopped together for the ring.

Her head had been in the clouds with her own relationship and battling how to deal with Lizzy's boyfriend confession. She suddenly thought she had been selfish with the time she had devoted to Tommy's life. Up to that point she'd always known everything about Tommy, but he had become a little mysterious and paying more attention to his grooming and she had become preoccupied at the same time. She had been focussed on her burgeoning relationship with Ryan and had forgotten to question further the most basic information about Tommy's relationship. Could Tommy's relationship and Lizzy's relationship be one and the same?

'What's her last name?'

'Lizzy Jones,' came Tommy's reply. 'But it will be Murphy when we get married.'

'And Lizzy's favourite colour is?'

'Red.'

Molly had been grasping at straws. Narrowing it down and hoping with each question she would find something that didn't match, but it all matched. Perfectly. She collapsed back in silence onto her wooden chair. Her eyes closed as tight as her chest felt at that moment. And to make matters more complicated, Ryan had helped to buy the ring for his own daughter. The daughter he didn't want to be going on dates, let alone getting married. The secret that Molly had hoped would go away had just got so much worse. It all seemed so overwhelming. How she wished Lizzy had not confided in her, but she had.

Molly wanted to be happy for Tommy, but her mind was torn between being excited for him and the potential for an emotional roller coaster of the worst kind playing out in her mind. The carriages were about to be flung off unless Lizzy told her father everything. Immediately. He couldn't find out second-hand. It would be the worst way for him to know and it would bring back too many painful memories of being shut out of his daughter's life before. Another father, in a different situation with no previous trauma, could deal with a hidden boyfriend, but with Ryan's past a hidden fiancé would be a recipe for disaster.

Lizzy was the sweetest girl and Molly felt sure that she and Tommy could be happy together, but only if Ryan accepted it. If not, then he could, with the best protective intentions, tear them apart before they had a chance.

But now Ryan had to be told that Lizzy not only had a boyfriend, she had a fiancé and not just any fiancé, Molly's brother. Which Molly doubted Lizzy knew. Nor did Tommy know, apparently, that Lizzy was the daughter of Ryan. They hadn't made the complicated connection. Molly was the only one who knew the whole story. Everyone else knew bits but not everything. So, who should really be the one to tell him? Her thoughts were becoming more jumbled by the moment. Layering one problem on top of the next and then sandwiching questions in between until she had a giant, precariously tipping sponge cake of trouble.

There were so many ways to look at the

problem. And then there was the ever so small chance it wouldn't be a problem. Perhaps Ryan would think it was a lovely coincidence and be happy for the couple. Unfortunately, Molly didn't believe that for a moment. After everything he had been through, being the last to know something that involved Lizzy was not going to sit well with him. Someone needed to tell him immediately.

But who?

Lizzy?

Tommy?

Molly?

Nothing in her head or her heart was making her feel confident about a happy outcome for anyone. It was already two weeks after Lizzy's confession so it probably wasn't going to help him with his trust issues as she had kept something about his daughter from him. But if she had broken a promise to Lizzy, how would that fare for any future relationship with the young woman, who might now be a part of her family? And poor Tommy might be caught in the crossfire and have his heart broken if Ryan tried to stop them seeing each other. The idea of them ever being a happy family was further from her grasp than she'd thought possible.

She was going to let someone down. It was just about picking the person she hurt.

* * *

Molly picked up the telephone. She could see it was Ryan's number. With bated breath she answered.

'Hello.'

'Hi, Molly. I was wondering, at the risk of becoming a nuisance, if you might enjoy lunch here at home with Lizzy and I in a few hours. You could bring Tommy along too. Finally, they can meet. And then later tonight I can have you all to myself when we enjoy our candlelit dinner.'

Molly swallowed the lump that had formed in her throat. If all four of them were in the room together it stood the chance of being the meeting from hell. She could picture it in her mind. Lizzy and Tommy saw each other and within a minute started holding hands and kissing. Ryan would be more confused than any man had ever been. And then it would all come pouring out in the worst way possible.

No, Molly knew she had to delay the meeting until Lizzy had confessed. She wondered if perhaps she could speed up the process by taking Lizzy aside and encouraging her to tell her father. If it came from Lizzy, then he might just accept it.

Molly wasn't convinced, but it was the most logical scenario.

'I'd love to have lunch with you but I don't think Tommy will make it this time.' It wasn't a lie; Tommy wouldn't make it because Molly would omit to invite him until she had spoken with Lizzy. Woman to woman, she would explain the value in sharing her good news with her father. And even if it wasn't accepted as good news initially, he might warm to the idea.

But Lizzy had to tell her father before he found out.

Just before twelve, Lizzy caught a cab to Ryan's house. She insisted so he gave her the address again in case she had misplaced it since the shopping expedition. Tommy was watching television when she left home and she promised to be back before dinner. He had a corned beef sandwich, an apple and a glass of milk and he was happy in his room as the weather was still dismal outside. He said he would call his fiancée some time during the afternoon because they had plans to make.

Molly just hoped she could manage the situation that afternoon so Tommy still had a fiancée at the end of the day.

'Come in.' Ryan greeted Molly with a tender but brief kiss as she wiped her feet on the doormat and stepped inside. Ryan's home was a hundred-year-old gentleman's bungalow. The cab had driven in the sweeping return driveway to drop her at the front door.

Ryan's mouth returned to hers and lingered after he had closed the door on the cold breeze. She felt safe in his embrace but also feelings of guilt were building. It could all be so temporary if she couldn't get Lizzy to tell her father what he deserved to know. It couldn't wait six months for Christmas.

'I'm so glad you could come over but I really wish you would have let me come and pick you up.'

'Honestly, there was no need.' Molly felt her heart racing and hoped that Ryan did not pick up on her anxiety.

'Let me take your coat,' he said as he pulled away slightly. 'I'll hang it up for you…'

'Molly!'

Molly turned to see an elated Lizzy skipping down the hallway to her.

'I haven't seen you all morning and you only come out of your room because Molly's here,' Ryan said, laughing. 'Well, I know where I stand.'

Molly felt Lizzy's arms wrap around her waist as she leant into her. 'I like you, Molly.'

'And I like you, Lizzy. I'm so happy that I get to spend the afternoon with you both.'

'Me too.'

Ryan hung Molly's coat on the ornate hall stand. 'Would you like to come into the sitting room? I lit a fire a few hours ago and it's nice and warm.'

Molly nodded and followed behind with Lizzy, as Ryan led them down the hallway. The home had been restored perfectly, or perhaps maintained over the years rather than restored. The dark antique furniture was pristine and looked stunning against the off-white carpet. There were modern paintings in the hallway, which worked as they were framed in an older style. It was like a picture from an elegant homes magazine and a long way from the home she shared with Tommy.

'Please take a seat and I'll put the soup on to warm and we can have a casual lunch on our laps in here.'

'Yum,' Lizzy said, rubbing her tummy. 'What soup?'

'Sooty dropped over home-made minestrone soup yesterday.'

'I like Sooty's soup.'

'I know,' he told her, then disappeared into the kitchen. 'I'll only be a few minutes.'

Molly sat on the sofa nearest to the open fire and Lizzy sat right next to her. Molly looked down and suddenly her worst nightmare was realised. Lizzy was wearing the engagement ring that Tommy had picked with Ryan's help.

Molly thought she might have a heart attack.

Molly sat staring straight ahead in contemplated silence. She could bolt from the house claiming a fake emergency; she could confess everything to Ryan; or she could hope that Lizzy told her father. But with all of the options, Molly couldn't hide from the fact that she knew. All of it now.

And well before Ryan had any clue.

'I've got another secret. Shh. I'm engaged.'

'Uh-huh,' Molly replied, and added softly, 'Have you told your father yet?'

'Has she told me what?'

Molly almost jumped from her skin. Ryan was standing behind them holding a small table for each of them.

'As I said, it's so cosy in here I thought we could sit and eat our soup and chat in here,' he continued as he put down the two folding tables in front of Lizzy and Molly. 'What's the secret? Do you want to go shopping together again?'

Molly sighed. His question was so sweet and naive. She wished with all her heart that a shopping date were all that Lizzy was hiding.

Before Lizzy had a chance to answer Ryan froze on the spot. His body went rigid and

Molly could see his eyes were focussed on the engagement ring on Lizzy's finger.

'Lizzy, is that a new ring?' he asked, moving the small tables out of the way before bending down in front of her. His voice was not raised but it was firm and coloured by concern.

'Yes. It's pretty.'

'And who gave you that ring?'

'My boyfriend.'

'It's a pretty ring,' Ryan replied with a hint of recognition in his eyes.

Ryan then shot a sideways glance at Molly. She could see that the pieces were falling into place in his mind and by his expression they weren't landing favourably. She knew he would have recognised the ring. How could he not? He had helped to choose it.

'It's beautiful,' Lizzy said with a beaming smile as she twisted her finger to hit the light and make the tiny diamond sparkle.

'I didn't know you had a boyfriend, Lizzy. What's his name?' Ryan's voice was calm and in no way threatening but Molly knew behind the calm there was a storm brewing. And she suspected the storm was heading her way.

'Tommy. He's nice. He asked me to marry him.'

'Tommy? Well, that's a surprise.'

'He's my secret boyfriend. Only Molly knew.' Lizzy giggled as she smiled up at Molly.

Ryan's glance at Molly was no longer sideways. It was face to face and more intense than Molly would have thought possible.

'I need Molly to help me in the kitchen with the soup, Lizzy. You can stay here in the warm room and we'll be back in a minute.'

Ryan did not need to ask Molly to follow him. In silence, she stood and walked behind him to the kitchen. Nervously she smoothed her jeans as she walked. There was no purpose in her actions but the adrenalin surging through her body forced her to do something with her hands. He closed the door behind them and stared at her in silence for the longest moment, then turned away and looked out of the kitchen window, still not saying a word. Molly suspected he was trying to choose his words but she didn't think any of them would be something she wanted to hear.

Finally, he turned back to her. His eyes were cold and unflinching, at odds with hers as they blinked nervously. The tension in his jaw was clear. His voice was a loud whisper with anger and disappointment both simmering close to the surface.

'You knew about this?' he started and then, without waiting for any response, continued.

'When did you decide to set your brother up with my daughter?'

'I didn't set them up,' she responded at a similar volume, aware that Lizzy was in the next room.

'You expect me to believe it was a coincidence?'

'It was. I didn't know that my brother and your daughter worked together. I just found out this morning that Tommy had proposed to Lizzy. I didn't know he was her boyfriend. I didn't know who she was dating but I didn't think for a minute it would be my brother. It just never occurred to me.'

Ryan rubbed the back of his neck. 'Not that I do believe you but, even if I did, you're still admitting that you knew she was dating someone and you didn't think I should know that? I'm her father. I should have been told.'

Molly chewed the inside of her cheek. That part of his rant was true and his anger with the situation was justified. Molly should have told him and would have told him under different circumstances.

'It wasn't my place to tell you.'

'Why not? You couldn't have been blind to my feelings about Lizzy dating. Didn't you think I should know something as important as that?'

'Yes, I know, but Lizzy had sworn me to secrecy. I couldn't break her trust.'

'That is so convenient. Such a tidy way to round it all up.'

'It's the truth.'

'I'm not so sure I can believe that word coming from you.'

Molly couldn't help but notice he wasn't using her name. He was keeping the conversation impersonal.

'You let me help your brother choose my daughter's engagement ring without knowing it was for her. Did you think for a moment that was okay?'

'I didn't know it was for Lizzy. You have to believe me.'

'I can't. It all seems way too convenient. I'm not blaming Tommy or Lizzy…'

'Great, so you're blaming me…' she countered, her hands on her hips.

'No, actually I'm blaming myself, Molly.'

She shook her head. 'Now I'm really confused. What have you done?'

'I've been too preoccupied with work and St Clara's…'

'Me?'

'Let's leave it there. I think you know where I stand on all of this.'

'Lizzy's nineteen, Ryan. She's not a child.'

Ryan rubbed his forehead in frustration. 'Lizzy isn't like other nineteen-year-olds. She has an innocent way of looking at the world…'

'As does Tommy. They are two wonderful souls who met each other and fell in love.'

'Do they really know what love is?' Ryan countered. 'Do they truly understand what marriage is all about? It's a lifetime commitment. It's more than a ring, a kiss and setting up home.'

'Don't sell Lizzy short now. From what you've told me, and Lizzy's outlook on life, you've never done it before. You've always encouraged her and never limited her. You've always been there to support her. Don't stop now when she needs you the most. They're engaged and I don't think either would be expecting this reaction to their happiness.'

'Can you tell me, when did my daughter confide in you? On your shopping trip?'

'No, actually it was my first day on the job. When she arrived for her appointment.'

'You expect me to believe that Lizzy told you this secret within minutes of meeting?'

'She did. And it surprised me too. I only agreed to keep the secret because I didn't know you were her father. I had no idea. I thought her father was parking the car or delayed. How could I have known when you have different surnames?'

'It doesn't add up to me. You made a promise to a young girl you barely knew.'

'To a young *woman*, not a girl, a young woman who wanted to confide to another woman about something she held precious. There's a difference.'

'Precious? They barely know each other either.'

'Nor did we, and I thought what we shared was something precious.'

Ryan looked down at the ground in silence for a moment. 'We got that wrong, didn't we?'

Molly felt her heart sink.

The door swung open without warning. 'You are talking a lot. Is the soup ready? Tommy will call me soon.'

'It will be ready in a few minutes, sweetie. You stay in the warm room and we'll both be right out.'

Lizzy disappeared back into the sitting room, leaving them alone. Molly didn't think there was any more she could say.

'I think I should leave.'

Ryan nodded. 'That would be best for everyone.'

'I'll talk to you on Monday when you have

calmed down. Unless you'd prefer I didn't come back to the practice.'

While she was effectively offering him her resignation, she hoped he would see that was not necessary and that they could work it out between them.

Ryan turned back to her, staring for the longest moment.

'Maybe you're right. It was only a four-week assignment and I'm happy to pay you out for the next two weeks. You can get on your feet and find something suitable.'

She couldn't help but notice he looked sad more than angry and that broke Molly's heart further. She really had messed up everything.

CHAPTER THIRTEEN

Ryan's new office manager, Gemma Potts, arrived bright and early on Monday morning. Molly had called the agency and said she wasn't feeling well enough to continue the assignment and needed a replacement.

Ryan acknowledged the young woman briefly and then went about his business of seeing the patients Molly had booked in on Friday, along with those that the automated booking system had booked in over the weekend. The week passed slowly and the nights even more slowly. He was angry with himself for being naive and allowing himself to trust again and for being too busy to notice what was happening in his daughter's life. He barely knew Molly and yet, for some now unfathomable reason, he had thought she was someone she wasn't. He was angry for almost falling in love with her.

He couldn't deny to himself that he felt

empty but that was how it had to be. He had to concentrate on Lizzy. He would cut back his roster at St Clara's to one night a week, and pay a locum to call in the other two nights. He might not be able to deter Lizzy from seeing Tommy in the future, but he would not be encouraging it. They had other issues at hand. They had to decide on the treatment plan for her and if that did or didn't include surgery.

It was three in the afternoon on Friday when George rushed into the practice, demanding to see Ryan.

'I left two messages for you,' George told Ryan when he appeared in the waiting room.

'I'm sorry, Dr McFetridge. I didn't want to interrupt your last patient,' Gemma offered apologetically.

'That's okay. I'll take it from here.'

'What's wrong with you? You should have returned my call,' George said, waving an accusatory finger at him.

Ryan could see the older gentleman's blood pressure was on the rise as he walked him into a consulting room and sat him down. He was sure he knew the reason.

'George, I can see you're upset.'

'Dorothy's in hospital.'

'I know, George. I'm so sorry. The doctor at

the Eastern Memorial called me late yesterday with the news. I'll be calling in today after I finish here.'

'But she wasn't sick, she was fine and not having her stupid cakes. I don't understand what went wrong.'

'It was a stroke. No one could have predicted it, George, but Dorothy's a strong woman and she'll pull through this.'

'She has to. I love her. I even love her stupid cat. I know I'm not the easiest man to live with but I love her and our family with everything I have. I wish I'd told her that more often. I think my military upbringing made me a hard man but Dorothy made me the best version of myself. She made me see that there's always two sides to everything. I know I stressed her at times, but she always found a solution to every problem. I'm not as cluey as her. I can't live without her. I'll stuff up everything with the family. They already think I'm a grumpy bastard and probably only tolerate me because they love her. They have no idea how much I love them. Women are so much better at the messy stuff than us.'

'Sometimes,' Ryan replied to George's ramblings, then asked him to take off his jacket and roll up his sleeve so he could take his blood pressure.

'You know, it's hard having daughters too. I have four of them and I swear they've always spoken to their mother about everything. What are they going to do without her?'

'You're thinking too far ahead, George. By all accounts Dorothy will recover. I'll see her tonight and get an update and I'll call you.'

'But if she's not okay the girls won't cope. They can't talk to me about the stuff Dorothy manages. They've all had so many secrets over the years and they knew their mother would hide that stuff from me and just deal with it.'

'You were okay with them hiding things from you?' Ryan asked.

'Sure, it's a woman thing. Girls need to confide in someone they think will understand and that's always another woman.'

Ryan thought about George's comment but wasn't convinced. His situation was different he tried to tell himself as he noted the blood pressure. As he became concerned with the reading, he changed the subject. 'You're one-fifty over ninety so we need to get that down. Make sure you take your antihypertensive medication this evening and I'd like to see you again tomorrow.'

'Sure, Doctor. Dorothy normally arranges that and I guess I must've forgotten it today.'

'You can't forget medications, George, particularly your blood-pressure tablets. You're a grown man and you need to take some of that responsibility away from Dorothy. When she gets home...'

'If she does.'

'No, George, *when* she does. As I said, there's no indication that Dorothy won't recover, but she'll need rest and you need to step up and take charge of running the house a little.'

'Running the house? I wouldn't know where to start,' George admitted, shaking his head as he rolled his sleeve down and slipped his tweed jacket back on.

'Then, George, you need to find out. And in a hurry.'

Ryan drove home that night thinking about George's remarks, but Lizzy had Ann; she didn't need to confide in someone she barely knew. But then he had also confided in someone he barely knew and made love to that same someone, he reminded himself. Taking a deep breath, he brushed those thoughts aside as he turned into his driveway. He had to let it go. He had to let his feelings for Molly go.

Ann was waiting with Lizzy when he got home. She had a small leg of roast lamb in the oven for the two of them to enjoy. The smell of rosemary sprigs on the slowly cooking meat filled the house.

'I'll be off, then,' she said. 'The potatoes and pumpkin are in with the meat and the gravy's in a small pot and the string beans are already in the steamer.'

'Can't you stay and have dinner?'

Ann smiled. 'Thank you for asking but I have bridge tonight. I have a few newbies coming along to my class. I do love it and they have a lovely supper for us so I won't go hungry. But don't forget to turn on the heat under the saucepan and it will all be ready in ten minutes.'

'What would we do without you?' Ryan replied as he dropped his jacket on the arm of the sofa.

'You'd manage, but I'm just grateful I get to see so much of Lizzy and you. It could have been so very different and I'm just so happy we worked through everything.'

'That makes two of us,' he said, nodding. 'So where is that wonderful daughter of mine?'

'In her room. I was going to speak to you about Lizzy tomorrow. She seems quite down at the moment. She mentions Tommy and Molly a lot, and I understand you want her to take things slowly with him. You did explain the boyfriend situation and the marriage proposal, and I know it was all a bit messy the way it came out, but she misses Molly terribly. I never met her but she sounds very nice.'

'Well, she's gone and we have to move on.'

'Pity, a young woman needs another woman to talk to at times. You might need to perhaps arrange a lunch for the two of them because she really is very sad not being able to see her.'

Ryan walked with Ann to the front door. 'I think Lizzy can confide in you quite enough, and I've lightened my workload so I'll be having more time at home, so she can open up to me whenever she needs. There's not so much happening in her life that she needs to find someone else to share the load.'

'Quite the opposite, actually. She's worried about the thought of the hysterectomy and wanted to chat to Molly about it.'

'She said that?'

'Yes. Lizzy doesn't want to talk to me or Tommy or you about it. Perhaps let them chat on the phone. She said that the pain is bad and she wants to have the operation. She is quite sure she doesn't want babies as they cry and they're messy, so she doesn't mind that she won't be able to have them, but she's a bit scared and she wants to talk to Molly about it.'

'I don't understand how she formed such a strong bond with her so quickly.'

'By the sound of it, you did too, didn't you?'

'It wasn't anything serious.'

'I might be seventy-six, but I'm not silly. I know when a man has fallen in love and is still in love, and that's you. You can choose to say it never happened but I can see it in your eyes.'

'It was just one night,' he replied, rubbing his neck. 'A fling, nothing more. It didn't work out.'

'I don't think it was a fling. I know you've had many flings over the last seven years, but Molly wasn't one of them. There was more to it than that. It can be as complicated or as simple as you make it, Ryan.'

'She kept something from me. And you of all people know I've been lied to in the worst possible way before and she did the same.'

'I don't know any such thing, Ryan,' she said. 'Tell me, who was she protecting?'

Ryan stood up and walked to the window and pulled back the heavy drapes to look out at the night sky.

'What do you mean?'

'You're punishing Molly for protecting the person you love most in the world by keeping her confidence. Molly risked her relationship with you to make sure she didn't let down Lizzy. She behaved like any mother would, under the same circumstances.'

'That's a romantic version of the situation.'

'No, it's the realistic one. Lizzy needs a mother figure, Ryan. She's at that age when it's important to be able to share things with someone closer to her age, not with her grandmother.'

'She can share them with me…'

'She can't. You won't accept that she is a young woman who wants the chance to love and Molly accepted that. And didn't judge her.'

'Her life is full without the complications. What if she gets her heart broken? How will I heal that for her?'

'That's what this is really about, isn't it? You want to protect Lizzy. Well, you can't, and shutting Molly out is making four of the sweetest people in the world suffer because of the actions almost twenty years ago by of one of the most selfish women in the world. You and Lizzy were both hurt by my daughter and I can see her for what she was then and still is. She has the life she wanted and she doesn't want her past to ever interfere with her new family. She knows that you have custody of Lizzy and can't understand why you would want to adopt her. Madeline doesn't have a selfless bone in her body and her deceit ruined lives and robbed us all of Lizzy for a long time, but you can have everything your heart desires now if you just let go of the past. She hid a secret to benefit herself, not to protect anyone else. There's a big difference.'

With that, Ann stood up and walked to the front door and prepared for the cold weather that would hit her when she stepped out to her car. 'I love you, Ryan, like you were my own son, so I have to be honest. You, and you alone, are the only one standing in the way of everyone being happy. Including yourself. Stop trying to protect Lizzy from people who love her…and stop protecting your own heart from feeling the same happiness.'

Ryan didn't put the heat on under the string beans that night. Instead he sat in the dark for an hour thinking about everything Ann and George had said. He hated to admit it at first but, alone in the darkness, he soon realised they were both right. He had been hiding behind the pain. Pushing Molly and Tommy away to protect Lizzy, when in fact his own actions were hurting her more. While he didn't have the power to change the outcome for himself—he had single-handedly ruined that—he knew he had to make things right for Lizzy and Tommy.

It was late at night when he drove to Molly's house with Lizzy in the car. He had explained to her that Molly was Tommy's brother on the drive over and that they were going to visit them. He also explained that since they were unannounced they might not be able to stay, but that he wanted to try. When he pulled up, he left Lizzy locked in the warmth of the car and, unsure of what he would say and how Molly would react, he walked up the front path. He was taking a risk, but he had been a fool. He had brought the hurt from the past into his present and ruined everything wonderful. There was no one else to blame but himself, he knew, as he knocked on her door. While Tommy and Lizzy would have their struggles, Molly was right in wanting to support them.

'What are you doing here?' Molly demanded as she opened the door. Her emotions were still raw and she did not invite him in out of the chilly night air. Instead she pulled her dressing gown across her chest and stood her ground against him and the icy cold breeze.

'I'm here to apologise and let you know that you were right.'

'I'm confused, Ryan. Where's this sudden change of heart coming from?'

Her brow was wrinkled and her eyes squinting in his direction and he didn't blame her for her reaction.

'What you said and did, all of it came from

your heart, from pure intentions. I just couldn't see it.'

'A week ago, you told me you didn't want to see me, you showed no desire to support Lizzy and Tommy's relationship, oh, and that's right, let's not forget you fired me.'

'I was stupid and there is no excuse for what I did.'

'Yes, you were, and no, there's not. So, if that's it, goodnight.' With that Molly half-closed the door.

'Wait, Molly. Please hear me out.'

'Why should I?'

'For Lizzy and Tommy's sake…and for us.'

Molly flinched. 'Us? I trusted you, I let you into my heart and you threw that away. There is no us. It was over before it began.'

'No, it began and it was real for both of us. There has never been anything more real to me than what we shared that night. But if it's over for you, then I will understand and re-spect your decision, but you need to under-stand why I did what I did,' Ryan said, not taking his eyes away from Molly for a second. 'I've spent the last seven years feeling guilty for not being there for Lizzy. The thought of my baby daughter being alone in the hospital and then being adopted when I should have been protecting her from the moment she was born has driven me to protect her at all costs. I didn't want her to get hurt like that ever again.'

Molly lifted her chin and took a deep breath. 'But I would never hurt Lizzy, not for anything in the world.'

'I know that. I was just scared if she fell in love she would get hurt and I worried you were encouraging her to be in love. Not that there's anything wrong with that anyway.'

'I wasn't encouraging her, I was supporting her. And being hurt is part of life, Ryan.'

'I know, and you were strong enough to risk that hurt when you put your trust in me that night in...our hotel room.'

'Well, that was a bad decision on my part.'

'No, it wasn't, in my mind. My knee-jerk reaction was the bad decision. You did everything you could to make everyone happy. I didn't know how to deal with the idea of my daughter falling in love. It scared me to the core but the way I reacted was wrong and what you did was right. I've realised that I've been an idiot and, while I thought I had put the past behind me, in fact I was still hiding behind it and using it as a shield.'

Molly looked past Ryan, still unsure what to think. 'Is there someone in the car?'

'Yes, Lizzy's out there. I'm hoping that you will allow her to see Tommy and she's excited to see you. She's missing you both so badly and nothing will cheer her up. If you slam the door on me and choose never to forgive me, I would understand. And I'd deserve it, but, please, can you consider allowing Lizzy to stay here with you for an hour or so. I can go and come back later.'

'You want Lizzy to spend time with Tommy?'

'Yes.'

'And me?'

'Yes.'

'So, you approve of their engagement, then?'

'Yes. Tommy's a wonderful young man. There was never any doubt in my mind about that. And, by how unhappy she is without him, I know she loves him too.'

Molly turned her head to listen to what he had to say.

'There's no guarantee they'll survive the challenges ahead. I know now they both deserve a chance at love and our support. And Lizzy wants and needs you to help her make a very big decision. It's a woman's issue and I would appreciate if you would talk that one through and perhaps meet with her specialist if you have time. A father can only do so much.'

He stepped back a little to give Molly space to think.

'Are you sure about all of this? Really sure?'

'I have never been so sure. If you would see Lizzy and let her see Tommy too, then one McFetridge would be very, very happy.'

Molly looked at the man standing before her. She could hear the honesty and anguish in his heartfelt words. She hadn't fully understood the guilt he had been carrying for seven long years. She had assumed it was anger and bitterness, but she had been wrong. Guilt had been driving him and he should never have felt any level of guilt. None of what had happened to Lizzy had been his fault. He had done nothing wrong up until now. And he wanted to make what he had done wrong right again for everyone. He was taking the biggest risk, reaching out and putting his trust in her...and in Tommy.

'And what would make the other McFetridge happy?' she asked with her head tilted slightly.

Ryan looked at her standing in front of him, with her hair a gorgeous mess around her beautiful face and a dressing gown that had seen better days hiding the body he had loved that night they had shared together.

'I would be the happiest man alive if I could have you back in my life. Not for a night, not for a month, but for ever. Waking up to your beautiful face every day and telling you how much I love you is all I will ever need.'

Molly drew a deep breath and stepped from the warmth of her home into the warmth of his arms and the beginning of her fairy-tale ending. With her lips only inches from his, she muttered, 'Then I guess you need to bring Lizzy inside and there will be *two* happy McFetridges tonight…and for the rest of our lives.'

* * * * *

If you enjoyed this story, check out these other great reads from Susanne Hampton

White Christmas for the Single Mom
Twin Surprise for the Single Doc
A Mommy to Make Christmas
A Baby to Bind Them

All available now!